At Risk

At Risk

Jacqueline Guest

James Lorimer & Company Ltd., Publishers
Toronto

First publication in the United States, 2004

James Lorimer & Company Ltd. acknowledges the support of the Ontario Arts Council. We acknowledge the support of the Government of Canada through the Book Publishing Industry Development Program (BPIDP) for our publishing activities. We acknowledge the support of the Canada Council for the Arts for our publishing program. We acknowledge the support of the Government of Ontario through the Ontario Media Development Corporation's Ontario Book Initiative.

The Canada Council | Le Conseil des Arts
for the Arts | du Canada

ONTARIO ARTS COUNCIL
CONSEIL DES ARTS DE L'ONTARIO

Cover design: Clarke MacDonald

Canada Cataloguing in Publication Data

Guest, Jacqueline
    At risk / Jacqueline Guest

(SideStreets)
ISBN 1-55028-847-4 (bound).—ISBN 1-55028-846-6 (pbk.)

I. Title. II. Series.

PS8563.U365A8 2004   jC813'.54   C2004-904206-8

James Lorimer & Company Ltd., Publishers 35 Britain Street Toronto, Ontario M5A 1R7 www.lorimer.ca	Distributed in the United States by: Orca Book Publishers, P.O. Box 468 Custer, WA USA 98240-0468 Printed and bound in Canada

For Tyler,
who loves to sink his teeth
into a good book!

The author would like to thank the staff of
the Project 118 Youth Ranch for
their help in the research of this book.
Thanks also to Sue McIntosh of
Healing Hooves Equine Facilitated
Counselling and Brenda Sourisseau for
their guidance on the handling of horses.

Chapter 1

The white-hot July sun seared Tia Winter's eyes as she scanned the road for the prison bus. A salty drop of sweat ran down her forehead and she swiped at it absently. Staring at her hand, Tia saw it was trembling. "Stop it! You can do this," she scolded herself.

"Hey, are you okay?"

Tia jumped, unaware she'd spoken out loud. It was Tyler Simmons, a fellow counsellor. "Ah, sure, I'm fine. I was just thinking that this girl I have as my first client is a tough case. Sage Knowles is a runaway and a convicted thief, not to mention the little problem with drug addiction. Pretty scary stuff." As a new counsellor at the Circle Four Ranch for troubled teens, Tia desperately wanted to do a good job, but she felt the pressure of being a rookie.

Ty smiled reassuringly. "She fits the profile of most of the girls who come here. Stop worrying,

Tia. You'll do fine. Besides," he teased, "I read in her file that Ms. Knowles isn't actually addicted to drugs; she only uses them for recreation."

Tia rolled her eyes. "Great, that makes me feel a whole lot better." Ty was her mentor at the ranch. He had years of experience as a social worker for girls at risk, and she was grateful for any advice he could give.

She looked around at the corrals, barn, and pasture, and then at the Alberta Rockies towering over them. "I think it's cool that this is an actual working ranch with the counsellors and clients running it. If I were a runaway from the street and was sent here instead of a juvenile facility, I'd be a happy cowgirl."

"You were raised on a farm, right? So all this must come naturally." Ty swept his arm to encompass the entire ranch.

Tia nodded. "Which is why the roping and riding part of this job doesn't scare me. It's trying to get through to a teenaged client so I can help her that has me, well, a little bit worried." This was the understatement of the century, but Tia didn't want Ty to know just how nervous she was. "I know how to handle horses; I understand them and can usually convince them to do what I want. The idea of failing with a horse is bad enough, but failing some kid whose future is in my hands really kicks it up a notch."

Ty seemed to understand how she felt. "Keep in mind that the girls who come here are actually the lucky ones. Sure, they'll work hard physically doing chores like fencing, tending livestock, and handling horses. But it's good for them, and you can do a lot of thinking while sitting in a saddle driving a herd of cattle. They'll also receive tons of praise for their efforts. Remember, with these kids, positive feedback for a job well done is not part of their daily life pattern."

He picked a long blade of grass and stuck it between his teeth. "And remember, it's not all ranch chores. They have schoolwork too — which is a big shock for kids who are dropouts."

Tia knew that was a key component in ensuring these girls succeed. The Circle Four philosophy was that both the body and the mind should be healthy.

"With your background, you'll love this part." Ty hooked his fingers in the pockets of his jeans and grinned at her. "At the Circle Four, we like to refer to ourselves as *trail riders*, not counsellors. It helps the girls shift into a ranch frame of mind."

"*Trail riders* — sounds downright horsy!" Tia drawled with a smile, her tension starting to ease.

Her eyes swept the far hills once more. The punishing heat made the horizon shimmer in a wavering haze. Suddenly she saw a telltale plume of dust, and her heart began to race. The prison transport from Calgary was on its way.

Tia stood calmly waiting. With his rugged good looks, a tailored Western shirt, and designer jeans that fit his slim build perfectly, he looked like an ad out of *Modern Rancher*.

"I'm a little freaked out," she shrugged, embarrassed but feeling the need to be honest. "Okay, a *lot* freaked out. At university, I read the reports and wrote the papers, but this is the big league, Ty, not a case out of a textbook. The Circle Four is the last chance for these girls. If we fail, they go back to life on the street with drugs, prostitution, and no future. You know the chances are high of them ending up with a lousy stint in jail, or maybe even dying because of some creep drug pusher in the next dark alley. I want to make sure these girls never end up in a dumpster with the police checking their dental records for identification."

"You can't focus on the negative, Tia. Don't psych yourself out before you've met this kid. You're part of our team and we'll be there for you," Ty smiled encouragingly, "*I'll* be there for you."

With a quick check into the distance, Tia saw that the pale dust cloud had drawn closer.

She wondered if Ty was right and she was sabotaging herself before she'd even started. In the past, there were times when, real or imagined, she hadn't felt accepted by her classmates. She'd been a loner, but not by choice. She hadn't fit in. After all, there weren't many black Canadian farm kids in rural schools, and she'd stuck out. She always wondered if it was this difference that made her an outsider, always looking in.

A picture of her kid sister flashed into Tia's mind. Katy with her *problems* that required help twenty-four hours a day. Poor Katy was alone too.

Other kids never wanted to play with her. Tia had been the only one who could see past her sister's twisted body and angry outbursts to the beautiful person who hid inside.

An orange flash emerged from a stand of pines, catching Tia's eye. The bus.

A young woman with a tanned face and a battered straw Stetson walked over to join them. "Ready for the next round, cowboy?"

Ty winked at the newcomer. "You bet your saddle and boots. Sara Johnson, I'd like you to meet Tia Winter; she's our new trail rider."

Sara shook Tia's hand. "Welcome to the Circle Four. We heard all about you at the weekly meeting. You come with super credentials." She bobbed her head toward Ty. "Don't let this tall drink of water scare you. The girls are a little rough on the edges, but they usually come around in no time."

"That's good to know." Tia smiled at the friendly trail rider with what she hoped was confidence. She supposed it was natural for a new employee to be discussed among the staff, but it did add to her nervousness.

Sara picked up on Tia's agitation. "Don't worry, the first one is the toughest. If you need help, Ty is always ready with advice. In fact," she laughed, "he'll be giving you advice even if you don't want him to." Waving, Sara left to talk to another trail rider.

When Tia looked back at the road, the transport

had disappeared into the dense trees again. She sighed. Sara seemed so confident and at ease, like she'd done this a million times before. She didn't look that much older than Tia's nineteen years!

Ty tossed the piece of grass he'd been chewing on. "I know this is scary, but with your academic background and horse expertise, no worries. You're going to do a top-notch job and, come this fall when you head back to that fancy university of yours, I'll be the first one to write you a recommendation."

Tia appreciated his pep talk and hoped Ty's faith in her wasn't misplaced. The problem was that, from what she'd read about Sage Knowles, being successful might prove a tough job. "Sage has already struck out three times in court, and the social worker who sent her here thinks the next time she screws up, the judge should put her in a Young Offenders Centre and throw away the key. That's the part that makes me nervous." Tia knew she sounded unsure of herself and hated it.

Ty hesitated, considering his answer, and Tia noticed that his thick brown hair curled at the collar and would need a trim soon. When she looked into his hazel eyes, the flecks of gold seemed to float freely in them. Her own were as plain as walnuts and the same dark brown colour.

Under any other circumstances, she might wish Tyler could become more than her mentor, but she was here to work and wouldn't be distracted, even by eyes like his. He wiped his neck with a red-checked kerchief. "In a lot of respects, these girls are like horses. They don't trust easily and will test you every chance they get. You have to pass their tests before you'll be able to get close enough to break through. Staying one step ahead and beating them at their own game is all part of the job."

"That's why I think the Equine Facilitated Counselling Program here is so great!" Tia said excitedly. "It teaches young people how to understand a horse, communicate with it. Once a teen can do that, miracles like trust and self-confidence happen. I think one of the big problems kids from the street have is lack of communication skills. It's hard to ask for help when you can't find the right words."

Equine Facilitated Counselling was why Tia had applied for the position at the Circle Four. The program was perfect as it combined her two very different passions — psychology and horses. She couldn't have dreamed up a better job if she'd tried!

The bus broke through the trees, and with a loud grinding of gears, the noisy vehicle rumbled over the cattle guard and moved laboriously up the driveway.

Ty laid a hand on her shoulder. "I think Sage Knowles is going to get a first-class trail rider."

They stood silently together in the hot sun as the weary bus ground to a shuddering halt.

"Sage Knowles, here I come." Tia whispered as she squared her shoulders and stepped forward to meet her client.

Chapter 2

The prisoner transport bus began to discharge its human cargo. As each girl's name was announced and checked off by the policewoman who accompanied the group, her assigned trail rider stepped up. Tia saw Sara Johnson greet her client, a tall girl with bright red hair.

Nervously, Tia smoothed the crease on her new wool pants. The itchy material made her legs feel like she was being bitten by hungry ants. Instead of her usual working clothes, the T-shirt and jeans that were suited for ranch chores, today she'd tried to dress like a professional, to look the part. She'd put her curly black hair up and added makeup to look older, then finished off with a crisp white blouse. Tia worried her height — almost six feet — and lanky build made her look like an awkward adolescent herself and would ruin her carefully prepared image. She hoped Sage Knowles wouldn't see through her disguise.

The steady stream of teens continued to clamber down the steps. The girls were all sizes and shapes. One new arrival with stringy mouse-brown hair was extremely overweight. Tia wondered how the girl would handle riding a horse or how the horse would handle the girl.

"That's Emma Harris," Ty said as he watched the large teenager look around apprehensively. "She's my project for the next few months. Wish me luck!" Ty started toward his client and Tia watched him smile warmly as he introduced himself. Emma smiled back sweetly and they went to retrieve her suitcase.

The glare on the windows made it impossible to see who was still on the bus, but when the parade of girls abruptly halted and Tia still had not seen Sage Knowles, she wondered if her client had missed the transport.

But if that had happened, why hadn't anyone notified her? There would have been time. Ty had told her the bus had been on the road all day and had taken a twisted route to the ranch to make it harder for the passengers to figure out exactly where the Circle Four was located. He said this ensured the girls had a sense of isolation and helped them come to grips with the fact that they would have no option to leave.

There was a sudden commotion on the bus and Tia could hear someone shouting. "Come on, come on. Move it, Madonna!" A large policewoman emerged dragging a reluctant girl behind her.

15

With a sinking stomach, Tia knew this must be the missing Sage Knowles. The petite girl was no taller than five feet and appeared not sixteen years old, which her file said, but more like thirteen. Her shoulder-length blonde hair was straight and fell across one side of her delicate face. She looked like a member of a church choir, not a hardened teen with a criminal record.

Her clothes, however, were totally from the street. No teenage girl would be caught dead in Sage's bag lady ensemble. She had on worn cargo pants with at least a dozen pockets, an army surplus flak jacket complete with a regimental flash on the shoulder, and a sweater that was old when Sage was born. In contrast to her Goodwill chic, hanging from a thick hockey-skate lace around her neck was an expensive looking digital camera. The tiny device glinted in the afternoon sun.

Tia remembered reading that the first thing you should do with a new client is to try to establish rapport. She could do that. She'd get close to Sage, forge a bond of trust. She felt the sheen of sweat on her forehead and wiped it with her sleeve. The fine powder kicked up from the horses' hooves had coated her face and her damp forehead left a dark smear on her snow-white blouse. "Oh, this *so* bites!" she fumed, irritated at the grimy smudge.

Tia moved to intercept her new charge before the policewoman had a chance to announce her name. "Sage Knowles?" she asked brightly.

Sage turned huge periwinkle-blue eyes to her, then sullenly thrust out her chin. "You were hoping for Ashanti?"

Tia blinked, taken aback. She wondered if Sage was making a racial slam, then decided this was the first of the tests Ty had mentioned. Not rising to the bait, she answered coolly. "No, Beyoncé actually." She stuck out her hand. "I'm Tia Winter, your trail rider."

"*Trail rider?*" Sage scoffed, then looked at Tia's outstretched hand as though it was an alien tentacle. She raised her small camera and snapped a quick shot of Tia. "Look, I don't do the touchy-feely thing." She tucked the camera inside her sweater.

Folding her arms across her chest, Sage tipped her head and glared at Tia. "And you can skip the phoney chit-chat. Let's get something straight. I don't like the idea of being your lab rat while you run whatever head games you learned in school this semester, so you can forget about pretending to be my buddy. I didn't pick this hole. My bogus social worker says I've got to be here." She turned abruptly to get her belongings.

Tia felt her face grow hot at how close to the truth Sage had come. Speechless, she watched her new client walk away. She noted that, while the other arrivals had large, bulging suitcases, Sage had only a small beat-up backpack. This girl travelled light.

Sage unbuttoned her frayed coat, then picked

up her pack. Walking over to the meagre shade afforded by the corral fence, she slumped lazily against the rails.

Her back ramrod straight, Tia followed. She quickly tried to think of something to say to get them back on the right track. Peeking out from under Sage's flak jacket, a distinctive gold pin shaped like a dragon caught Tia's eye. "Hey, that's a cool brooch."

Sage glanced down at the pin. "Yeah, I boosted it from some tourist trap when I was in Banff. I was gonna fence it to buy dope, but I kind of like it."

Tia stared at her, speechless. She couldn't believe how casually Sage had admitted this. Sage grinned as though she'd scored a point in some game they were playing where only she knew the rules.

Tia could have kicked herself for being so easily knocked off balance, but she hadn't expected Sage to be this outspoken about the details of her life. Realizing how much she had to learn, Tia vowed not to make that mistake again.

It was time to change subjects to one Tia was more confident with. "I've got a surprise, Sage. How'd you like to meet your new best friend?" Sage looked at her as though she was dealing with the most boring person on earth, then reluctantly followed Tia toward a large fenced field.

At the edge of the pasture, Tia climbed through the rail fence and invited her new client to do the same. "Don't worry, it's safe."

Sage had pulled her tiny camera out to snap some shots, but now stopped as she saw four horses cantering in the lush grass. "No way!"

Tia, who'd been walking toward the horses, turned back in surprise. She had imagined Sage, a city girl, would jump at the chance to be with real live horses. What kid didn't love a pony? "I thought you'd like to meet the horse you'll be riding while you're here."

Sage glanced at the frisky horses as though they were the most unappealing creatures on earth, besides ranch counsellors. "Well, you thought wrong. Sweaty, stinky horses are not high on my list of *must-haves*." She spun on her heel and started back toward the parking lot.

Tia watched Sage's small, retreating form. With a sigh, she clambered back through the fence and hoped she hadn't taken on more than she could handle.

Chapter 3

Tia knew she had to do some fast damage control. So far she hadn't been very successful, but now the velvet gloves were off. Quickening her pace, she strode past the arrogant girl. "Since we're going to be bunkmates, I'll show you where we live, then I'll give you the rest of the tour. Follow me."

Sage looked like she was going to make another scathing comment, then simply rolled her large eyes. "Whatever."

They walked down a red shale path leading to a group of cabins sheltering under some tall evergreens. The summer had been particularly scorching and the air smelled of dry grass and sun-soaked pines.

Tia kept telling herself that she was in the driver's seat and could handle the situation. "The ranch is set on several sections of land and has saddle horses, cattle, dogs, and at least a dozen barn cats; not to mention chickens, two goats, and a miniature donkey. As you figured out on the drive here, it's located in a remote part of the Rocky Mountains and the nearest town is a couple of day's walk over the toughest terrain in the world."

Sage didn't look up as she trudged behind Tia. "Sounds like a challenge to a runner like me. Hey, if it's such crappy land, how can you raise cattle?"

Tia was surprised at this insightful question. It was one she'd asked herself when she'd come here. "Good question. I found out there are large pastures scattered throughout the area, and the cows are split into manageable herds so they can forage without overgrazing."

"Let me guess who looks after these *manageable herds*." Sage grimaced. "Do I look like a friggin' cowgirl? Ditch that. I don't do smelly bovines!"

Tia ignored her blustering. "Home, sweet home." She indicated a small log cabin with the name *Larkspur* on a wooden plaque. Taking a key out of her pocket, Tia pulled open the screen door she'd painted bright red two days before and unlocked the weathered inner one.

The rustic cabin had one main room with a small airtight stove for cold mountain nights, a pine table and chairs, two plain dressers, and a small closet beside a set of bunkbeds. There was also a slightly cramped adjoining bathroom. The place was immaculate — beds meticulously made, no clothes showing anywhere, and the freshly polished table empty except for a laptop computer. Beside the laptop was an old jelly jar with a bouquet of wildflowers wilting in the stifling heat.

Tia thought she'd made the cabin look inviting, and hoped Sage would feel welcome. She nodded toward the beds. "You get the top bunk."

Sage stood at the door and looked up at the bed suspiciously. "Trapped on top, huh? Is that in case I have any thoughts about leaving without saying goodbye?" She wrinkled her nose in distaste. "Unbelievable! Does this four-star dive have electricity? I won't even ask about air conditioning. That was obviously an option you didn't spring for." As she took a step into the room, her face grimaced sourly. "Man, talk about cruel and unusual punishment."

Tia's patience began to wear thin. The heat was intense and her blouse had become soggy under the armpits. In defence of the cabin, she strode across the room and flipped on the light in the small bathroom, then shut it off with a sharp snap of the switch. "You can unpack later. Come on, I'll show you the other high points you'll need to know about."

Thinking she would speed things up, Tia reached for Sage's shabby backpack. The second she touched the strap on the pack, Sage snatched it away violently and hugged it tightly to her chest. "Back off!" she growled, her eyes feral.

"I was only going to put it on your bed." Tia

said softly, as she deliberately pitched the tone of her voice lower to sound soothing. It was the tone she used with a spooked horse, and she hoped it would have the same calming effect on this scared girl. She watched Sage unconsciously edge toward the doorway and freedom.

Flight response, Tia thought, remembering the term from her classes. She held her hands up. "I respect your privacy, honest. Just trying to help."

Sage relaxed as she moved toward the beds, her bravado restored. "I'm a little touchy about my stuff, that's all. I don't like anyone messing with it."

Not wanting to make Sage feel cornered, Tia stepped back outside, where the bright sunshine made her blink. Sage followed silently behind.

Locking the cabin door, Tia was about to slip the key back into her pocket when she stopped. She handed it to Sage. "You keep this. I can see you're a little worried about your valuables. That's understandable. I'll get another from the administration building."

Sage looked down at the small brass key in her hand, then up at Tia. "Is this a joke? Who ever heard of a jail where the prisoners have the keys?"

"This is not a jail, Sage. You're here because you're in trouble and have run out of options. The ranch was designed to be a safe house, a place to catch your breath and figure out what you want to do with your life."

The disbelief on Sage's face made it obvious

she was skeptical. Then she shrugged and tucked the key into the pocket of her threadbare cargo pants.

Turning, Tia walked along the path, explaining the rules as she went. "You have to tell me where you are at all times. I also need to know if any of your family will be visiting you."

"Yeah, like that's going to happen real soon," Sage muttered sarcastically.

As they continued the tour, Tia pointed out different buildings in the complex and laid out the rules. "No smoking, cell phones, drugs, or alcohol. And absolutely no fighting with other girls. This ranch is your only hope, Sage, and I want you to stay, but a violation like fighting will have you on the next transport to the Young Offenders Centre. This is a working ranch with lots for everyone to do."

Sage practised her bored face. "Man, lighten up!"

Tia stopped in front of a large log structure. "This is the ranch administration building, *admin* for short. It's off-limits unless you've been sent for, which usually means you're in trouble." She gave Sage a meaningful look. "And we don't want that."

Sage snorted derisively. "*We* don't, huh?"

This wasn't going like Tia thought it would. She took Sage to a building marked *Education*. "Rise and shine at six-thirty, feed and water your horse, breakfast, then classes here," she nodded at the building. "That's followed by ranch chores, supper; then tend the horses again, homework, and bed. Come on, I'll introduce you to your teacher, then we'll go to the barn."

"It sounds like heaven," Sage grumbled as she followed Tia into the school.

Tia left her with the teacher and headed for the admin building to pick up a key and all the paperwork involved with her new client. She would have to write both a daily and weekly report, and these would be used to evaluate whether the Circle Four was working for Sage Knowles.

The building was busy with trail riders and support staff as she walked in. Going straight to the locked cabinet, Tia used her passkey and grabbed one of the two spares marked *Larkspur*. She spotted Ty at a corner desk working on his own documentation, and headed over.

Ty tossed his pen down on the stack of papers. "Lots of red tape to plough through. I never was any good at dotting *i*'s and crossing *t*'s. It's the one drawback to an otherwise perfect job." Slouching back in his chair, he put his hands behind his head. "How's it going with Miss Knowles?"

"Unbelievable! I blew my credibility in record time." Tia flopped into a chair opposite the desk and proceeded to recount the incident with the dragon brooch. "… I thought complimenting Sage on the pin would help me connect. Instead, I came off looking like what I was — a complete rookie trying to make brownie points. And what's worse

25

is, I just don't get her. The way Sage talked about her life on the street, you'd have thought it was normal."

Ty raised one eyebrow. "Tia, for her it is normal. Remember, you're brand new to all this. Real life doesn't always follow what the textbooks say. Before I left the Ravenhill Institute, I worked my tail off to help a runaway. I thought I had her turned around, when there was a theft and my client was convicted. She swore she didn't do it, but the evidence was solid. I had a lot more experience then than you do now, and I was still totally taken in."

He folded his arms across his chest. "Sometimes you have to accept the fact that a girl can't be helped, no matter what you do. In our job, we don't like to believe the old adage that a leopard never changes its spots, but some of these girls resist. Don't be too hard on yourself if your flesh-and-blood client doesn't respond like a theoretical example out of a textbook. I had a look at Sage's file. She has a long record of shoplifting, starting at thirteen. You know she's here for boosting an expensive leather coat, and if the social worker hadn't stepped in, Sage would have ended up at the Young Offenders Centre. Sage isn't the worst-off girl here, but you have to be prepared for some disappointments — maybe even on your first case."

With a sigh, Tia stood. "You're probably right. I guess I thought it would be different. I'd better collect my paperwork. Hey, maybe we could have coffee later and, you know, compare notes to make sure I don't screw things up any worse?" Tia hoped she didn't sound desperate.

"Sorry, Tia, but no can do. Emma's bunking in the Bluebell cabin with Sara's new client, a girl named Meagan Dion. We're exchanging some babysitting time. Sara has to go beg her banker for an extension on a loan, so I said I'd show both girls how to clean stalls. Later, Sara's going to watch Emma for me. I have a meeting in Calgary and won't make it back until after dark. Don't worry." He straightened up and smiled. "You'll do fine."

"Thanks. Maybe coffee another time." Tia picked up the armload of forms and started back to the school and her second round with Sage. She thought about what Ty had said. She didn't like to think of Sage as a lost cause. Tia hoped no one so young could be that messed up, but either way she was about to find out.

Chapter 4

"How'd it go?" Tia asked, as she and Sage left the school.

"Like it always goes for me in school. It sucked." Sage looked sullen and very unimpressed. "The teachers are idiots and none of them can teach their way out of a wet paper bag."

The bitterness in her voice was unmistakable.

"Your file said you dropped out. More bad teachers?" According to the social worker's background check, Sage's parents were quite affluent, and it didn't seem likely she'd attended a second-class school, but Tia wanted to hear what her client had to say.

"No, it was me," Sage said matter-of-factly. "I guess you'd say I'm plain old stupid. I ended up here, didn't I?"

Tia was again taken aback at her blatant honesty. "You know, I've been reading a lot about the way people learn, and it can be totally different from one person to the next. For example, some students are visual, which means they have to see something for themselves in order to get it. Others need to repeat things over and over until it sticks. I mean, give yourself a break. Maybe your school used the wrong approach for you."

Sage didn't respond. Instead, she hung her head and fiddled nervously with her camera, avoiding Tia's eyes. Her body language screamed serious lack of self-confidence, but that was hard to believe from her tough *I can handle the whole freakin' world* talk. Tia wondered which was the real Sage Knowles.

* * *

The small barn was cool and dim when Tia and Sage walked in through the weathered wooden doors. Dust motes danced in the shafts of golden sunlight that slanted down through the high windows. The familiar aromas of hay, oats, leather, and horses blended into a wonderful earthy scent that filled Tia's nostrils. Barns were a sanctuary to her, and she loved the way they made her feel totally serene.

"*Horse shit!*" Sage exclaimed loudly as she clamped her hand over her nose. "It smells gross in here!"

Despite herself, Tia laughed. "The stalls are mucked out everyday," she said patiently. "Caring for your animal is an important part of your time here. Get used to it. Once you are assigned a horse, its food, water, grooming, and exercise will be entirely your responsibility. No one else will pick up after you or do your work. You'll clean out the stall daily and put your own tack away."

Sage looked at her blankly.

Tia realized her client had probably never ridden before, let alone dealt with the myriad items needed to take care of the animal. "*Tack* includes saddle, bridle, halters, grooming tools, and, well," she smiled, "all things horsy." As she was speaking, Tia glanced into a stall where a tall bay gelding was busily eating his ration of oats. Someone had left a hoof pick and sweat scraper perched on the wooden rail. She retrieved the tools and held them up for Sage to see before returning them to the tack box on the bench outside the stall.

"Don't worry," she continued. "I'll show you how to do things, then it's up to you." Tia motioned to a small room at the far end of the barn. "That's the tack room, where bigger items like saddles are stored." Frowning, she hung up a bridle that had been left draped across the gate of another stall.

Sage, who had been busy taking pictures again, stopped, then tilted her head. "Let me get this straight. You said everyone has to pick up after themselves?"

"That's right. Everyone is responsible for their own horse and tack."

"And this tack stuff includes junk like you put back in that case," she nodded toward the tack box where Tia had returned the pick and scraper. "And that leather thingy you put on that peg over there." She motioned toward the bridle.

"Yes, as I said." Tia wondered what she was getting at.

A smirk crossed Sage's delicate face. "Then how come you're picking up after the slobs who left that junk lying around?"

"I wasn't," Tia replied automatically.

"You were so!" Sage held up the camera so Tia could see on the view screen a series of miniature images of her bustling around the barn picking up the items and putting them away.

Tia hadn't realized what she'd been doing, and now felt a little embarrassed. Sage simply didn't understand. "Well, I … Because this area has to be kept clean and whoever left those things screwed up," she said defensively.

"It seems to me that I can leave my stuff lying around and you'll come along and clean up. I guess that makes you — not a housemaid, more of a …" She frowned in mock concentration. "*Horse* maid!"

"Very funny." Tia didn't like being goaded. "If you'd been listening instead of being a smart aleck, you'd have heard me tell you everyone …"

"Yeah, yeah," Sage said smugly and climbed up to sit on the stall rail. "You *said* everyone looks after their own junk, but that's not what you *did*." She looked down at Tia and waved the camera containing the incriminating pictures.

"I simply didn't want tools left lying around."
Tia could feel her face becoming hot. Sage had a
valid point, but she couldn't stand it when people
left the place in a mess. Having tools strewn about
was dangerous, and besides, it made her crazy.
She quickly changed the subject.

"This barn is too small, but we're hoping to
build a bigger one with our Raise the Roof project.
The ranch has been working on collecting enough
money to start." Tia rubbed the nose of a particularly striking horse. "This is Blaster. He's a
ten-year-old Appaloosa. You can tell that because
of his unusual markings — the dark coat and white
rump with black spots. He's mine." Tia could hear
the pride in her voice but didn't care. She believed
in being proud of yourself for a job well done, and
raising a beauty like Blaster was a lot of work.
"Okay, now that the introductions are over, I'll take
Blaster out to the pasture and then give you a quick
run through in cleaning out a stall."

"Is that what the well-dressed stable hand wears
to deal with horse pucky?" Sage nodded toward
Tia's white blouse and tailored dress pants.

Tia wished she didn't have the impractical
clothes on, but decided to brave it out. "Not usually, but since you're the one who's going to do
the shovelling, it doesn't matter how *I'm* dressed."
She went to the tack room and came back with a
halter and lead rope. Efficiently, she slipped the
halter on the big stallion and clipped on the lead.
"Coming, Sage?"

Sage took one look at the tall animal and shook her head. "That thing is two storeys high. No way I'm going near it."

Tia laughed. "You're right. He's tall for his breed and may have some mix in his background, maybe Thoroughbred since he's a full seventeen hands tall." She saw Sage's confused look. "A hand is four inches, so that makes him a touch over five and a half feet at the withers," she explained, pointed to the area above his shoulder. "We can do this together. I'll take him, you get the gates."

Looking extremely put out, Sage jumped down from the stall rail. "If you think I'm going to grovel in the slime everyday, you really are crazy. I told you, I don't do horses."

Sage continued to voice a string of complaints as they finished taking Blaster to the lush green field behind the barn.

When they were back at the stall, Tia handed Sage a pair of work gloves and held up a shovel and a manure fork. "Chose your weapon!" When Sage didn't move, Tia handed her the manure fork. "The dirty straw goes in that wheelbarrow and then outside to the compost pile. We hose down the stalls with disinfectant once a week. You finish up by spreading the clean bedding."

A look of disbelief crossed Sage's face. "Are you on cheap drugs? I'm not doing it!" Her voice was very loud and one of the horses whinnied shrilly at the unexpected sound.

"It's not up for discussion, Sage. It's part of your job here." Tia wasn't about to let a mouthy brat dictate terms to her.

"Is there something wrong?" Ty's voice from the door made both young women look around. He was standing with Emma and Meagan Dion, Sara's client, and all three were watching Tia and Sage.

"No, not at all." Tia tried to sound like everything was completely under her control. "Sage is going to clean out Blaster's stall and can't seem to get motivated, that's all." She folded her arms and looked pointedly at Sage.

Sage gingerly held up the manure fork and gloves, then dropped them unceremoniously into the dirty straw. She glanced at Tia, then turned to Ty.

Her voice was soft and child-like when she spoke. "Actually, Ty, I'm allergic to horses and if I clean out this stall I could go into anaphylactic shock. My throat could swell up and I'd die."

Tia stared at Sage, who had somehow managed to look small and helpless as she stood in the large wooden horse stall. She suspected the "little girl lost" act was well used by this master manipulator.

Sage continued, "I tried to explain to Tia, but she wouldn't listen. She says I have to do it even if it makes me sick."

When Sage coughed theatrically, Meagan groaned. "Oh, pul-ease!"

Emma giggled.

"Sage, you should be in the movies." Tia folded

her arms. "I read your file. You are *not* allergic to horses. In fact, you have no allergies at all, except maybe to honest work."

Caught in the lie, Sage glared at Tia and strode out of the stall.

Ty walked over, picked up the manure fork, and then took the shovel from Tia. "I don't mind showing you how this is done, Sage. Let me get Emma and Meagan started, then I'll be right back." He smiled warmly at the young runaway.

Sage leaned against the side of the stall and, casually slipping her camera out from under her sweater, shot the other two girls as they prepared for the dirty job.

"Wicked! I love all this Wild West stuff," Emma said enthusiastically. She smiled at Ty and headed for the stall at the back of the barn.

Tia glanced at Meagan and suspected from her denim shirt, faded jeans, and worn riding boots that she came from a ranching background. She was certainly dressed appropriately.

Meagan stepped forward and gave Sage the once-over. "Like you're some kind of freaking ballerina, too good to slop out the horse crap with the rest of us? Cut the B.S. and think again, Camera Girl."

"Drop dead, ditch pig!" Sage spit the words out.

"Skank!" Meagan fired back.

"Whoa, ladies! Focus," Ty interrupted before the two girls could come to blows.

35

Meagan turned her back on Sage and spoke to Ty, "Are there rubber boots in the tack room?"

Tia smiled to herself, her suspicions about Meagan's roots confirmed.

Ty indicated the door at the back of the barn. "You bet. A pair with your name on them."

Meagan, who stood a head and shoulders taller, moved past Sage, bumping her as she went. Tia saw Sage's eyes flash and her hands ball into fists. Quickly, she stepped in. "Sage, let's wait for Ty in the stall." Sage shot the tall redhead an acid glare, then followed Tia.

After showing his two girls how to muck out stalls, Ty returned to Sage. "Now, let's see what we can do. I'm sure you'll have no problem once you're shown how."

He sounded so positive, even Tia believed him. She was interested in what Ty was up to. She did not think it would be what Sage expected.

Picking up the shovel, Ty demonstrated how it was done. "I always like to start in the back corner and work my way forward." He scooped a hefty pile of dirty straw.

"Should the wheelbarrow stay outside or should it come into the stall?" Sage asked innocently, shooting Ty, his shovel loaded with muck.

"Oh, I leave it outside." He continued cleaning as Sage watched.

"And how do I get the clean straw back here?" she asked. Her tone sounded serious, but Tia saw the corners of her mouth tip up in what looked suspiciously like a smirk.

Emma and Meagan stole surreptitious glances at each other and Tia knew they were memorizing every word. Ty continued cleaning as Sage lounged against the side of the stall. Tia was becoming irritated. This had gone on long enough.

"Do you want to give it a try?" Ty asked Sage.

Sage looked like she wasn't sure which was the business end of her manure fork, then she started to fuss with the work gloves Tia had given her. Tentatively, she picked up a forkful of old straw. Tossing it in the general direction of the wheelbarrow, she managed to get only a handful into the device.

"Oops! I don't seem to be too good at this." She smiled sweetly at Tia, who had started to fume. "Could you show me a little longer, Ty?" She leaned on her fork and watched the tall trail rider continue to efficiently clear the soiled horse bedding. When he had nearly finished the job, Sage tossed another partial forkful a little nearer to the wheelbarrow.

"That's not quite right, Sage. I have two more stalls to clean. Come and watch me again." Ty instructed. Grinning openly at Tia now, Sage followed Ty to the next stall.

"You know, maybe it's the fork. Here, try my shovel." Ty handed Sage the implement. She picked up a small shovel of dirty straw and tossed it into the barrow. "I know this is hard, Sage. It's probably because you're so small and weak. You probably can't lift a whole shovel of this wet stuff. It takes a strong back." Ty scooped up a forkful and deftly shook off the straw leaving only the manure, which he deposited into the wheelbarrow.

Sage looked indignant. "As if! I'm not some freakin' wimp." She scooped another shovel, this one heaping, and tossed it expertly into the wheelbarrow. Then she stopped, and her face flushed as she realized what she'd done.

"Great! I knew you'd get the hang of it!" Ty congratulated her as he pounced on her mistake. "Now, you continue with these two stalls while I check on Emma and Meagan. You're surprisingly strong for such a petite girl." His compliment was lost on the furious teen.

Ty started out of the enclosure, oblivious to the daggers in Sage's eyes. Walking straight to the back stalls, he spoke to the two girls who were now busily tending to their own work, then re-joined Tia.

"Nicely done," Tia said. He'd handled the problem like a pro. "I know you have to leave for your appointment, but I'd like you to look at one of the fillies in the corral. She skinned her foreleg and I want to make sure it's not infected. After showing Sage how to clean so thoroughly, I'd say you can safely leave these last two stalls for her to finish." Tia turned to leave, then stopped beside the stall Sage was working in. "Laying down the new bedding is the fun part. I think clean straw smells wonderful."

Emma and Meagan overheard and snickered, then laughed out loud, hooting and braying.

Muttering curses, Sage glared at Tia and savagely scooped up another shovelful.

Tia moved away from the smelly wheelbarrow before Sage could toss the dirty straw in her direction. Accidents did happen.

Chapter 5

The next morning Tia was up at five o'clock to go for her usual ten-kilometre run. She felt edgy if she didn't get it in and was sure her muscles would turn to mush if she missed even one day. She'd been late getting to bed because it had taken her longer than she'd expected to finish the daily evaluation forms on Sage's progress. She'd been very careful writing it, making sure it sounded as positive as possible. As Sage wasn't the most positive person she'd ever met, Tia had done a lot of rewriting.

As she followed the path along the riverbank, Tia began to live in the rhythm of her steps. The air was like crystal, clear and sharp. She loved the way the mountains made her feel, as though she could fly, soar over their jagged peaks and look down on a world made perfect by her very distance from it.

After the incident in the barn, Tia had complimented Ty on his brilliant handling of the situation and had vowed to deal with the next altercation herself. Sage had been grim faced when she'd finished cleaning the two stalls. She hadn't spoken to Tia during supper and had gone to bed shortly after.

Returning from her run, sweaty but satisfied, Tia showered, then she and Sage went to the barn to feed and water Blaster. "The stalls looks great!" Tia hoped the praise would make Sage feel pride in her accomplishment. "You did a great job."

"Yeah, and Meagan hung around to watch the whole thing. She is such a witch." Sage turned away and practised looking bored again.

* * *

Ty and Emma were already seated in the dining hall when Tia and Sage picked up their breakfast trays and started over to their table.

"Morning. Pull up a chair," Ty invited. "You ready for the branding this afternoon?"

Emma, dressed in voluminous denim bib overalls, answered before either Tia or Sage had a chance. "I sure am. I've never been to a branding. It sounds like a blast." She rested her dimpled chin in her hand. "What happened next, Ty?"

Tia and Sage sat down as Ty launched back into the story he'd been telling Emma. "I worked with Old Slim on a spread near Denver, Colorado. He was deathly afraid of heights but didn't want anyone to know about. Now, you ladies may not know this, but Denver is known as the Mile High City because of its elevation above sea level. Every time that cowpoke climbed on a horse, he'd be sick to his stomach. Slim said it had nothing to do with the height of the horse, just the altitude of the pasture!" Ty grinned and finished his coffee.

"Jeez, you move around more than a dope dealer." Emma reached for the coffeepot and refilled her cup and Ty's. "You've travelled all over Canada and the United States, and have had some way cool jobs."

Tia could see the stars in Emma's eyes and made a mental note to warn Ty. He wasn't doing anything to discourage the obvious infatuation, and it could be dangerous for him. Girls with unrequited crushes could get male counsellors into serious trouble.

"I think I may puke!" Sage groaned, her pixie face screwed up into an expression of disgust. "I need some fresh air." She rose to her feet and took her tray to the service trolley next to their table.

Tia was about to follow, when Emma stood and waved at someone in the food line. Turning, she saw Meagan with her tray. Spotting the signal, the tall redhead immediately started toward their table.

As she passed Sage, Meagan stopped then sniffed. "Whew! I guess you couldn't get the stink out of your ballet slippers after all that *extra* shovelling you did yesterday." She looked down at

Sage's soiled shoes. "Next time, wear rubber boots and spare us all having to breathe your dung-scented perfume."

"You sure it's my shoes?" Sage retorted. "I don't see anyone busting a move to be close to you. Next time, try a shower before joining the rest of the human race."

Smiling sweetly, Sage waltzed past, giving Meagan's arm a well-aimed elbow as she went. The impact caused Meagan's tray to flip into the air, depositing the scrambled eggs in a greasy mess on Meagan's clean blouse.

Emma, who had been silently watching the exchange, gasped and stepped back from her egg-splattered friend.

"You rotten little ..." Meagan cursed loudly as she wiped a gob of sticky egg off her pants and started after Sage.

"I don't think so!" Ty, his voice curt, caught her by the arm and restrained the furious girl. Sara, waiting in the food line, rushed over and hastily tried to calm her client down. Tia hurried after Sage.

Sage never looked back.

* * *

The branding was set up in a corral on the far side of the barn. Holding pens held cows and their calves, and the air was filled with their nervous cries. By the time Tia and Sage arrived, there was a crowd of ranch hands, trail riders, and clients at their posts in the corral.

"Branding is crazy busy and everyone has a specific job," Tia explained. "It looks like mass confusion, but there is a system. The calves are let into one end of the corral and a cowgirl on horseback ropes an unwilling volunteer by the hind legs, then drags it toward the branding area at this end." She indicated a propane tank and heating barrel with branding irons in it. "The bulldoggers wrestle the calf to the ground and hold it until all the procedures are finished. I've done the actual branding before, so that will be my job and you'll help."

Sage stared in horror. "You've got to be kidding!"

Tia looked at her in surprise. "*Now* what's the problem?"

"You take a defenceless little animal and some bully holds it down, then you, you … *burn it!*" Her eyes were wild. "That's horrible! What about the calf? Does anyone ask it if it wants to be tortured like that?" Sage was frantic. "It's barbaric and I'm not doing it!"

Tia tried to calm her down. "Look, Sage, this is the standard way branding is done. We're fast and it helps identify the calf if it's lost. Anyone finding it can return it safely. We also ear tag them with special barcodes so they can be tracked their whole life wherever they're shipped. The whole thing is part of life on this ranch and every other cattle operation in the world!"

Tia handed the distraught girl a spray bottle. "I don't want to cause any more trauma than necessary either, so I insist on using that." Sage looked at the bottle quizzically. "It's aloe vera," Tia explained. "Your job will be to spray it on the fresh brand."

"Why?" Sage demanded, still upset.

"The aloe helps the brand heal faster, and it seems to stop the pain. " Tia pulled on her leather work gloves and walked over to the metal container where the irons were heating.

The idea of the aloe treatment seemed to mollify Sage and she gave the bottle a test drive by spraying a nearby fencepost.

Tia glanced at her and, seeing she'd calmed down, continued. "The entire process is like a choreographed dance. One ranch hand inoculates for black leg; another bug tags the ears with a fly repellent; then the wrangler in charge of implanting the growth hormone steps in. After that, we brand the calf and, if it's a bull, he's neutered."

Sage looked shocked again. "You mean they cut off his …"

"All part of life on a ranch. Hey, don't worry. That particular task isn't in our job description." Tia smiled at Sage. "Now, aren't you glad I volunteered us for branding?"

Sage gulped.

Everything Tia had described was standard on a ranch, but she could see how it might overwhelm a kid from the city. She thought back to a school lecture. Was Sage identifying with the plight of the calf? There was a distinct similarity between a helpless calf being cornered, overpowered, and physically assaulted, and a cornered teen being trapped and attacked on the street. Did Sage feel she was being kept a captive here on the ranch like these helpless cattle?

At a signal from the head bulldogger, a young First Nations cowgirl on a nimble-footed pinto approached the milling calves. With a deft throw of her rope, she selected the first candidate. Branding had begun.

As the day wore on, the unrelenting heat became intense. The dust kicked up by the horses and calves coated everything. It was hard work and by mid-afternoon Tia and Sage were exhausted and ready for a break.

Sage headed back to their cabin to tie up her sweaty hair, while Tia relaxed under the shade of a tall poplar. While she was enjoying a well-earned frosty drink, Ty walked up.

"It's going well." He pushed his Stetson back on his head.

"Yes, but a killer long day. My back had forgotten how hard branding is." Tia stretched, trying to work out a particularly nasty knot.

"I think it's important for the girls to join in. Working as part of a team is an important life skill they'll need when they leave here." Ty cracked the top on a can of soda.

"Ty!" Emma called as she pushed through the crowd toward them. "I wondered where you went." She was breathless and looked extremely pale.

"How are you holding up, Emma?" Ty offered her a fresh can of soda, which she declined.

"This isn't as much fun as I thought it would be," Emma answered weakly.

Tia could see the girl was nauseous.

"I found out what else is happening ... to the boy calves ..." Emma swallowed loudly.

"Castrations?" Ty asked. "It sounds gross, but fifty percent of these calves are bulls. A farmer invests tens of thousands in a good foundation bull and having half his herd capable of messing up his breeding program doesn't work." His eyes twinkled mischievously. "Besides, prairie oysters are a tradition for supper at a branding."

"I thought we were having chili and hamburgers, not seafood." Emma's brow wrinkled in confusion.

"Oh, prairie oysters aren't from the sea. You might say they're a *by-product* of a branding." Ty explained.

A look of comprehension came over Emma's face. Groaning, she clamped her hand over her mouth, turned, and fled in the direction of the nearest bathroom.

Tia gave him a dirty look. "You didn't have to tell her that, Ty. You could see she was sick."

"You're right, Tia. I shouldn't have teased her."

Ty finished his soda in one gulp. "But it's part of life here, life on any ranch, for that matter. Look, Emma's a strong girl and intelligent. I'm sure once she realizes how important and necessary it is, she'll understand."

Tia saw Sage moving through the crowd and waved. She looked so small compared to the other girls that Tia again marvelled at how she could have survived on the streets. She suspected her client was a more accomplished thief than her rap sheet let on.

"Hi," Sage said as she joined the trail riders. "They need to have porta-potties closer to the corrals if we're supposed to be here all day. The toilets by the admin building are jammed." She had a clipboard in her hand. "I was up there and Dr. Stone saw me doing nothing — which is what waiting to go to the bathroom looks like after fifteen minutes — and he asked me to bring this down for you to sign, Ty." She handed him the clipboard.

Ty looked at the forms. "Right, I asked to be off premises a couple of evenings and I guess our chief administrator wants to make sure the paperwork's done." He took a green pen with gold lettering out of his shirt pocket and signed the document. Tia squinted up at the hot sun and wished for a cool breeze. By the time she looked again, Sage was already headed up the hill, clipboard and pen in hand.

"After I return this, I'm going to check on the

calves to see if they've recovered from our brutal attack. I can still smell smoking cowhide." Sage started back up the hill to the admin building.

"I'll meet you back at the branding irons in twenty minutes," Tia called after her. Sage waved a dismissive hand and kept going.

"That kid's smooth," Ty said with an admiring shake of his head.

"What do you mean?" Tia asked.

"She boosted my pen!" He laughed and tossed his empty can into the recycling box. "I'd better get back to it. See you at the campfire later."

He tipped his hat and left, leaving Tia wondering at Sage's nerve and Ty's patience. She knew an important part of being an effective counsellor was to know which battles were worth fighting and which to walk away from. Tyler Simmons was a master at this skill.

A half-hour later, Tia had finished her break and was waiting in the corral for Sage, who was a no-show. Muttering about unreliable teenagers and ignoring the fact that she was one herself, Tia searched for her lost assistant. She checked the holding pens and surrounding field, then decided to have a quick look in the barn.

Entering the barn, she could hear raised voices. Her eyes took a minute to adjust to the darkened interior that, after the scorching heat, felt almost chilly. Rounding the corner of a stall, she stopped.

Emma was sitting in the straw watching Sage and Meagan square off against each other. Tia's eyes were immediately drawn to the branding iron in Sage's hand.

Meagan glanced over and saw Tia. Before Meagan's hands went into her pockets, Tia thought she saw something glinting in the dim light. "I'm glad you got here, Tia. Sage needs someone to tell her the irons are for the calves. She tried to attack me with one. She's crazy! I think she should be reported and sent packing." Meagan strode purposefully toward the door. "Someone should put a leash on her."

Tia looked questioningly at Sage. "What's going on?"

Sage shrugged. "Nothing I couldn't handle." She looked down at the branding iron in her hand. "It isn't even hot. I'd better get this back to the corral." Turning, she left Tia and Emma alone in the barn.

Tia helped Emma to her feet. She could see the girl had been crying. "Emma, what happened?"

Emma swiped at her cheeks. "After I found out about the oysters thing, I felt gross and came in here to cool off, but ended up puking my guts out. Meagan came in and started teasing me, so I told her to take a hike." She took a long shuddering breath. "Then she told me I was fat and lazy and that I shouldn't have been given the chance to come here. I told her to drop dead, then started to cry. Not because I'm a baby," she added pointedly, "but because I felt so rotten. That's when Sage showed up and told Meagan to back off. Then things sort of took a turn for the worse." Emma pushed her stringy hair behind her ear. "I think Meagan had a knife. When I saw Sage had the branding iron, I thought the two of them were going to kill each other. I'm glad you got here in time."

Tia remembered Meagan jamming her hands in her pockets when she'd come in. She hadn't actually seen a knife, but if Meagan did have one it would be a very serious offence. She helped Emma back to her cabin to rest.

It was frightening to know that the two girls could so easily go to such extremes. Even the suspicion of Meagan having a knife meant Tia had to tell Sara about the fight immediately. But she was sure that if there was a knife, it would conveniently disappear by the time Sara questioned Meagan. And without hard evidence, what could Sara do?

Tia also needed to tell Ty. Right now, it looked like Sage was the only one with what could be considered a weapon. Until they got to the bottom of this, the girls would have to be supervised when they were together.

Tia spotted Sara waiting near the corral and went to break the news.

"From the way those two behaved at breakfast, I knew it would only be a matter of time," Sara sighed. "I'd better get on this."

As Tia watched the trail rider make her way through the crowd, she wondered just how far Sage and Meagan would have gone.

Chapter 6

With the branding finished, everyone looked forward to a hearty meal, followed by an evening relaxing around a campfire. Except for tending to the horses there were no chores, for which Tia was grateful. Every muscle in her body ached, and she decided she would have to add weight training to her exercise program. She was totally out of shape!

Sage had gone back to their cabin to shower before supper, while Tia helped clean up after the branding then checked on Blaster.

Brushing dust and debris from her jeans, Tia could practically feel the extremely long, exceptionally hot shower she was going to take. Walking up to their cabin, she pushed open the door, then stopped dead in her tracks.

The cabin looked like a cyclone had hit it. Dirty clothes and wet towels were strewn everywhere, and less-than-clean sneakers lay in the middle of the floor.

"What the …" She looked up at Sage's bunk and her mouth fell open. Sage sat stark naked in the middle of her bed, smoking a cigarette. "What in hell's-half-acre do you think you're doing?"

"Drying off after my shower." Sage exhaled a long stream of blue smoke.

"Where did you get that cigarette? You know it's against the rules." Tia walked over and kicked Sage's manure-caked shoes outside, then furiously picked up the clothes strewn about the cabin and stuffed them into the laundry hamper in the bathroom.

"It's a reward for coming to Emma's rescue," Sage explained, inhaling deeply. "She told me where you trail riders stash your butts in the admin building and I helped myself. The locks on that place are really Mickey Mouse." She looked at Tia, daring her to deny the existence of the private supply of cigarettes.

Tia knew of only one trail rider who smoked. Ty had told her he was trying to quit, but from the evidence fouling the air in the cabin, he obviously hadn't beaten his habit yet.

Striding over to the beds, Tia reached up and plucked the offending cigarette out of Sage's fingers. "This," she held the smouldering butt up, "is not going to happen again." She threw it into the wood stove, then took a calming breath. "Sage, about this afternoon in the barn. I've told Meagan's trail rider there was a fight, *with an illegal weapon*, but that no one was hurt." Sage didn't

53

respond, so Tia pressed on. "I'm telling you here and now, you two have got to stop this. If you get hauled in front of Dr. Stone, he'll send you to the Young Offenders Centre to finish your time."

"Look, be cool. It was no big deal," Sage protested. "When I saw Meagan follow Emma into the barn, I figured I'd go see what the party was about. I learned a long time ago never to walk into a fight without protection. That's why I took the branding iron, but it was just for show." She swiped at a glowing ember that had fallen on the green woollen blanket. "I know I'll get hung out to dry. I'm the one caught with the weapon. I figured since I've already got one foot on spring ice and the other on wet soap, it wouldn't matter if I helped myself to a butt or two."

Tia's angry boiled over. "A branding iron could be considered *deadly force* if you planned to use it on Meagan's head! And it's not only you. Emma told me Meagan may have had a knife. So forget about playing dumb with me."

Sage flinched and Tia wished she hadn't used that particular phrase. She knew Sage was sensitive about her problems in school. Tia could practically see the girl close down and knew she'd get no more out of her. "Get dressed, I'm going to have my shower." Without another word, Tia strode into the bathroom and slammed the door.

Things definitely weren't improving. She felt like she was failing Counselling 101.

The evening meal was a well-earned reward for everyone at the ranch. The cooks really outdid themselves and Tia found herself going back for dessert.

"I never turn down food either." Sage followed Tia up to the buffet. "I've been hungry too many times."

The off-hand way she said it made Tia's heart contract. How many other kids were out there on the streets, hungry and miserable?

Back at their table, Tia soon found herself wishing she hadn't taken such a big piece of pie. But after what Sage had said, she felt guilty even considering ditching it. She took two more bites, then pushed the plate away. "I'm sorry, but I can't finish this. I may explode! Anyone want prime leftovers?"

Ty shook his head. "My tank's about full too. Man, this is really first class grub, wouldn't you say?" He looked inquiringly at Emma, who nodded, her mouth full.

Ty had told Tia he would escort Emma to supper as a way of making up for teasing her about the oysters that afternoon. The invitation had instantly restored Emma's appetite.

"That's my girl, Emma. You worked hard today. You deserve to give yourself a treat," he laughed, "or two!"

Emma flushed and swallowed with difficulty.

"I haven't had food this good since the last time my mom cooked for me. She really rocked in the kitchen." Emma looked at everyone's empty plates, then defiantly took a large bite of her blueberry cobbler. "I was taught never to waste food. There are kids starving in Somalia — or is it Suburbia?"

At that moment, Meagan walked by. "Especially if they're a citizen of your suburb," she sniggered and continued on.

Emma glared at her, but kept eating. "We'll see who has the last laugh, Miss High and Mighty."

"What do you mean by that?" Tia was alert to the smug tone in Emma's voice. Something was up.

"I don't think I thanked you properly for coming to my rescue today, Sage." Emma smiled slyly; there was no mention of the information about the cigarettes that she'd already shared. "In fact, after Ty gave me that little lecture on staying out of trouble, which I don't think I deserved at all…" She looked woefully at her hero. "I decided that maybe Meagan should have a taste of what it's like to be in hot water." She grinned conspiratorially. "I think Meagan's babysitter will be very interested when she reads the anonymous note left on her bed about a certain bossy girl who has in her possession an illegal cell phone."

Tia and Ty looked at each other. Tia was amazed at how quickly loyalties shifted between the girls. She thought from their behaviour the first day in the barn that Emma and Meagan were best buddies, but that alliance had dissolved at the branding. Tia frowned, remembering seeing Meagan stuff *something* into her pocket, but not actually seeing a knife. Emma had planted that idea in her mind. It could have been anything… "Meagan didn't have a knife, did she, Emma? It was the cell phone she stashed in her pocket."

"Yeah. So what?" Emma protested, her face going red again.

Emma's eyes slid down and to her left. *A classic guilt reaction*, Tia thought, remembering the chapter on body language she'd read first semester. Emma had deliberately lied about the knife.

Sage kept her head down and didn't say anything. Instead, she reached over and pushed Tia's left-over pie toward Emma's now empty plate.

Tia hoped Sara hadn't reported the alleged knife to Dr. Stone. Meagan would deny having it and sound like a liar. She couldn't say she didn't have a knife, a banned item, and then tell them it had actually been a cell phone, another banned item. It was a classic case of being caught between a rock and a hard place, and Tia had played a part in putting Meagan there. Tia would have to straighten this out with Sara.

Chapter 7

The next morning Tia decided it was time to introduce Sage to her horse. She'd need to hurry and get her client's horseback riding skills up to par. They were scheduled to move a small herd of cows to summer pasture in a few days and that meant a lot of saddle time.

Tia was waiting for Sage after her school session. She'd spoken to the teacher and been assured that, while Sage's progress was slow, she was an intelligent young woman. "How much experience have you had with horses?" Tia pushed open the big wooden doors to the barn.

Sage looked at Tia as though she were insane. "I went on a merry-go-round once when I was six. That's enough for me. Horses are big, smelly and dumb as a doormat."

Tia thought about this. "Oh, really? Come on."

Sage narrowed her eyes suspiciously, then followed Tia through an adjoining door into an arena where a round pen, fifty feet across with wire mesh walls eight feet high, was set up.

"Hello, girl," Tia murmured softly to the horse that stood quietly in the pen. "We have a non-believer here, so we need to show her what teamwork is all about." The horse snorted softly and blew out its breath. "Sage, this is Bouncing Betty. Isn't she pretty?"

Sage flopped down onto a bench beside the enclosure and yawned lazily. "Whatever. That fleabag looks like all the rest of the nags around here."

This was the behaviour Tia had come to expect — cool and aloof and not giving two cents for anyone in the world but Sage Knowles. Tia entered the pen. "Well, we'll see about that," she muttered under her breath as she grabbed the thirty-foot lunge line and lead rope hanging near the gate.

The quarter-horse mare watched her with wary eyes. Her reddish-brown coat was patchy and appeared dull, but her eyes were bright and alert. Tia moved slowly toward the old horse. "Betty, you and I are going to give horse whispering lessons to a real greenhorn, so don't let me down." The horse skittered nervously and moved to the far side of the enclosure, her ears pricked forward as she kept an eye on Tia. Sage continued to look bored, but Tia saw her attention refocus on the nervous animal.

"Betty is the perfect size, don't you think?"

Keeping her body square to the mare, Tia took a step toward the horse. Betty nickered and tossed her head, again moving away from Tia. Tia flicked the lunge line, gently tapping the horse's rear quarters, and Betty sped up a little.

Sage straightened, now openly watching the exchange in the round pen. "If you say so. She doesn't like you much. I think she needs obedience lessons."

Tia coiled the line and slung it over her shoulder, then took a step toward the horse. She stared directly into the mare's eyes, not blinking. Raising her arms slightly, Tia spread her fingers.

The horse reacted as if a tiger had suddenly sprung into the pen. Her head came up and her ears pointed directly at Tia. Tia could see the whites of the mare's eyes as the muscles of her neck tensed. The horse was ready to bolt. "You see, Sage, horses are prey animals, food for predators. They never forget that. She thinks I look like a cougar ready to pounce."

Sage stood up and moved toward the pen. Nervously, she watched the exchange. "Hey, stop that! Can't you see the horse is freaked out?" Her voice was anxious. "You're scaring her!"

Tia moved closer. Now that she was cornered, the horse shifted her posture to an aggressive one. Tossing her head, she laid her ears back, nostrils flaring as she exposed her large teeth. Although only slightly over fourteen hands high — her withers a foot below Tia's head — Betty looked imposing and quite ready to stomp something and stomp it hard.

"You should get out of there, Tia. *Biting Betty* looks ticked off." Sage's voice was almost frantic. "Pick another horse!"

Tia noticed the use of her name. "Actually, Sage, I picked Betty to be *your* horse." She emphasized the word *your*. This startled Sage so much, Tia heard her draw in her breath.

"You're kidding, right? No way I'm having anything to do with that monster." Sage took a step backward, her eyes wide.

Tia lowered her arms, then turned her body slightly away from the horse at an angle, no longer looking the mare in the eye. The horse immediately calmed down. Betty understood the threat was gone.

Tia knew the animal would rather be with the safety of the herd than alone, and that she didn't want to fight if she didn't have to. Despite their size, horses are delicate creatures and easily damaged. Being alone and cornered by a predator is a horse's worst nightmare. Horses are built to run, and their instinct takes them there first.

Tia saw that Sage was very frightened. She was freaking out, and it was understandable. Although the horse was big, Tia had terrified the animal when she'd trapped and threatened it. Sage, too, considered herself strong and in control, but on the streets, she was a target for anyone more powerful who could trap her in a corner. Tia remembered Sage's reaction to hearing about the branding. It was happening again.

It was exactly what Tia had read about in her books, and it unsettled her to see life confirming the theories she'd been taught. Tia could see that Sage's tough-girl attitude hid her fear and lack of self-confidence. She had very little control on the streets and, like a horse, would always be on the lookout for predators.

"Would you believe me if I said I could get Betty not only calmed down but following you around without a rope?" Tia moved to open the gate of the pen. "Come on, I'll show you how."

"Get lost." Sage's words caught in her throat. "I'm not going into that cage so some crazy horse can kick the crap out of me." She tossed her head, sending her mane of golden hair flying back over her shoulder.

Tia raised her eyebrows. "You're suffering under the delusion this is a democracy. It's not." She pushed the gate open. "Don't worry. I won't let you get hurt."

Sage didn't seem to believe her and glanced at the door to the barn. Tia caught the eye movement. She'd learned that when someone is cornered, they react with either *fight* or *flight*. As Sage edged toward the door, Tia figured she had about two seconds before her client booked, to use the street term Sage knew very well. She thought quickly. From the way she'd acted with Meagan, Tia knew Sage would never turn down a direct challenge. "What's the matter? Are you chicken?"

Sage's head snapped around at the insult. "As if." She sounded nonchalant, but Tia saw the tremor in her lips. With one last reluctant look at the door, Sage moved to the gate and slowly edged into the round pen.

Betty snorted and pawed the ground.

Sage blanched and Tia thought she was going to run after all, but instead the diminutive teen bravely stood her ground.

"I want you to move over here." Tia pitched her voice low. Sage took a tentative step forward. "Come and say hi to Betty." Together they walked over and stood beside the horse. Tia held the mare's halter as she rubbed the animal's wide forehead with the flat of her hand. Betty blew her breath out noisily, but accepted the attention. "Rub, don't pat. Go on, give it a try," Tia encouraged.

Sage hesitated, then stuck her chin out and, reaching up, rubbed the horse's nose. Her eyes grew round with surprise. "It's like velvet," she whispered as she stroked the horse. "And so warm." She stared at her hand as though she couldn't believe it was actually touching this huge beast.

"Great job, Sage!" Tia congratulated her client as they moved toward the rear of the horse. She handed Sage the coiled lunge line, being careful not to stand directly behind the horse where they could get kicked. "I want you to get Betty to run in a circle by gently pitching the lunge line at her rear quarters like I did earlier." Sage stood rigidly, holding the rope as though it was a king cobra. "You can do it," Tia encouraged softly.

Awkwardly, Sage tried a couple of false starts, then got the hang of it and nudged the horse forward. Betty cantered in a circle away from them.

"Keep looking straight at her. Move her forward with your line," Tia instructed as Sage glowered fiercely at the horse.

After a few more revolutions, Tia showed Sage how to make Betty change directions. Then she moved to the edge of the pen, leaving Sage in the centre. "Move her around again." Hesitantly at first, then with more confidence, Sage did as she was told.

"This is the tricky part," Tia called. "We have to convince Betty that she should vote you boss. I'm not talking about beating her up. Her instinct says if you want to play with her, be her friend, then you have to show her that you're worthy. Horses like to follow, not lead, but you have to prove you're up to the task of leading." Tia kept her voice low. "Watch her ear, the one closest to you."

Sage focused on the ear. "Hey, it's pointing to me and the other one's still moving around in circles. I didn't know horses could make their ears do different things at the same time. Wicked!"

"Betty is showing you respect by keeping that ear on you. Now keep watching. Next she'll probably chew and lick her lips with her tongue."

Betty obligingly did exactly that. Tia knew Sage was still very wary. "Coil your rope and look down at the sand — don't make eye contact — and I want you to turn your body away from her." Again, Sage did as she was instructed, but Tia could see she was terrified at turning her back on the horse. Her entire body was stiff and her eyes were squeezed tightly shut.

With a snort and a soft nicker, Betty moved a step closer, then another. "Yes!" Tia whispered triumphantly as Bouncing Betty gently laid her big nose on Sage's shoulder, her breath fluttering the loose blonde hair.

Sage's eyes flew open. She didn't move a muscle, stoically standing her ground.

"Super! Betty wants you to be her friend." Tia smiled. "Now, walk slowly around in a big circle and see if she'll go with you."

Sage took tentative step forward. Betty did the same.

Sage took another, longer step and Betty dutifully followed.

As Tia watched, Sage and the mare slowly walked around the pen in a solemn procession of two.

"Hey! She's staying with me!" Sage turned and Betty obligingly followed her back around in the other direction. "I'm making her do what I want!"

Tia was elated. "You sure are, and you did it without muscle or shouting. I think you'll make a fine trail boss!"

Sage's face split into a wide grin. She looked like a happy, normal sixteen-year-old girl for the first time since her arrival at the ranch.

They spent the next hour becoming acquainted with Betty, massaging her neck, withers, back, and flanks until both Sage and the horse were comfortable with each other.

"Okay, now you get to go for a ride," Tia announced.

Sage, who'd been working the horse in a figure-eight pattern, stopped so suddenly that Betty bumped into her. "No, I don't want to. Walking around with this big fur bag trailing behind is one thing, but getting up where she can run the show, that's a whole other ballgame."

"I'll help you. Don't worry. You're in a round pen, so she can't run far," Tia laughed. Sage was not amused. "Trust me, you can do this," Tia reassured her.

Sage didn't look convinced, but Tia proceeded to saddle the horse anyway. She knew that successfully riding a horse would give Sage a real feeling of confidence. Along with that, it would boost her self-respect. She would have accomplished something important.

Everything Tia had been taught about salvaging someone from the brink of disaster said the same thing. Sage needed to see herself as worthy, deserving more than she settled for when she was on the streets. She had to know it for herself.

Tia brought in the variety of equipment she'd

need. Gently, she placed a saddle pad on Betty's back, then the saddle. Next she tightened the girth and shortened the stirrups. Tia made sure she always moved in front of Betty, rubbing her nose as she went from one side to the other.

After she'd put the bridle on, she tucked the reins under the saddle. "Okay, now I want you to get Betty to walk around behind you again."

"I told you, walking is okay." Sage knew exactly what to do, and soon she and Betty were again doing laps around the pen.

When Tia was satisfied that both the horse and the prospective rider were calm and ready, she moved on to the next step. "Come on. I'll give you a leg up." Again, Sage hesitated and Tia gave her a meaningful look. "It's not an option." She moved to the near side of the horse where Sage would mount.

"Oh, all right! But if I get killed, I'm going to sue your butt off." Sage grimaced as Tia helped her climb aboard the horse.

Once in the saddle, Sage sat absolutely still. "This is not good!" She protested nervously. "I can't do this. I want off this freakin' nag."

Although her tone was tough, Tia saw Sage's lip quiver and knew she was scared. It was understandable. Although Betty was not a tall horse, it would seem like a huge distance to fall.

But Sage had come a long way in a short time. She'd gone from outright walk-away scared to challenging herself to overcome those fears, her trust and confidence climbing with each small step forward. Tia knew this was an incredible distance for anyone to travel.

"Sage, you've done the hard part. Betty likes and respects you. She'll do what you say." Tia looked up at Sage. "You can do this." Sage turned her huge blue eyes to Tia and Tia found it was like she was looking at a small child.

"Tia, I'm afraid." Sage's voice was a soft whisper.

Tia understood that to admit fear was an extremely hard thing for Sage to do. It meant she was not in control, that she was vulnerable and able to be hurt. Smiling reassuringly, Tia reached up and touched Sage's arm. "I won't let anything happen to you. I promise."

"What do I do next?" Sage asked, still not daring to move a muscle.

"First thing is to relax. You're going to spook the horse. Take five deep breaths." Tia watched Sage do this and saw her shoulders relax. "Good. Now I want you to hold on to the reins while I lead Betty around." Taking the halter, Tia walked the horse around the pen. "Keep the reins loose."

After bobbling a little, Sage got the hang of balancing in a saddle. Tia let go of the halter and slowed her pace.

Betty, who had done this whole exercise many times before, knew exactly what to do. She kept walking.

"Tia, I'm doing it!" Sage squeaked. "I'm riding!"

Tia could hear the excitement in Sage's voice and saw the wide grin on her face. "Keep going!" she called. "You're doing everything exactly right!" Horse and rider approached the end of the pen. "Okay, turn her. Neck rein left by moving your left hand away from her and letting the right rein contact her neck. Now, move your right leg back behind her girth and press on her side with your knee. Good! Keep your left leg against her so she pivots around that leg as she turns. Don't yank on the reins, use your knees."

"Jeez, who knew driving one of these things was so complicated." Sage screwed up her face as she concentrated.

Sage and her horse turned — a little awkwardly, but they turned. Tia smiled. "Great! You're a natural!"

They spent the next hour practising moving the horse until Tia decided both horse and rider were ready for a rest. "Okay. Time to cool off, have a brush and a bucket of oats for a job well done."

Sage giggled. "Do you mean Betty or me?" She fumbled in her sweater for her camera, holding it out to Tia. "Would you take my picture?" she asked, almost shyly.

Tia couldn't believe she was being offered the precious talisman. She knew that to Sage it was much more than just a camera. She took the small device, snapped the picture, and handed it back. "You look like a real cowgirl up there."

Sage fiddled with the mode switch on the tiny

camera. "When I left home, I cleaned out my bank account to buy this," she said. "I had the crazy idea about being a freelance photographer wandering the world and selling my award winning shots to National Geographic. That's why I blew my millions on this high tech model."

"Sounds like a career worth fighting for," said Tia.

"It was a stupid dream, that's all." Sage stuck her camera back in her sweater.

"A dream is the first step to your future, if you want it badly enough," Tia added smiling.

Sage didn't smile back, but for a fleeting instant, Tia could have sworn she saw hope in the teenager's eyes.

Together they took Betty to her stall for a well-deserved rest. Tia sensed something had changed in Sage. She seemed more animated, more confident. It was as though a small fire had been kindled that, with care, could turn into a blaze.

Chapter 8

Client Evaluation Log: Tuesday, July 27...

Tia stopped, pen poised over the paper. It was after ten, but this had to be done. She looked at the blank page. What could she say? *Sage Knowles responding well to ranch environment — she hasn't swung a branding iron at anyone in days!* Right, like that would look good in someone's case file. She felt out of her depth with Sage and had thought about getting a T-shirt that read *Duck! School doesn't prepare you for the front lines.* Quickly she jotted down "*Ms. Knowles has begun responding to the early phases of Equine Therapy.*" Translated, it meant she could saddle her own horse now. Tia worried that it wasn't clinical enough and decided she could always rewrite it later. She closed her logbook and turned out the light. Tomorrow was another day.

Ranch work was tiring enough, but add to that the duties of a counsellor, like writing never-ending evaluation logs and giving progress reports at the weekly morning meeting, and Tia found herself more exhausted than she could ever remember being. She had started to float into a well-earned sleep when Sage climbed down from the top bunk.

Deciding she must be going to the washroom, Tia turned over to avoid the light Sage would turn on. She couldn't believe how tired she was...

Tia drifted in her dream. The cabin door opened and closed. A cold draft swept over her. It felt so real that she shivered. Was it winter? She should get up and make sure the door was locked, but she was way too tired. She'd check it in the spring...

* * *

The next couple of days went by smoothly, and Tia thought she was starting to get the hang of the trail rider/counsellor stuff. She met Sage after her morning school sessions and they'd work together with Bouncing Betty. Sage started to voluntarily spend more of her free time with the old mare. From her study of Equine Therapy, Tia knew this was a very good sign.

One afternoon, while Tia and Sage were repairing a stretch of barbed wire fence, a never-ending chore on the ranch, Sage started to ask questions regarding Betty's care.

"I've been trying different junkfood out on the old girl. She's a pushover for black licorice." Sage hammered another staple into the wooden fence-post, securing a dislodged strand of the three-wire fence. "I used to hide a jar of the stuff under my bed at home."

Throughout the day, Tia had tried to get Sage to talk. Knowing her client disliked being crowded, she'd been careful to ask her questions casually, allowing Sage to answer as much or as little as she felt comfortable with. It had been exactly the right approach. Slowly, Sage had opened up and Tia felt as though there were at the beginning of trust.

Ty had told her that any kind of talking was important when it came to gaining the trust of a street kid. He'd told her that sometimes a client would ramble on about one thing, but would actually be talking about something entirely different, something much more personal that she couldn't discuss directly.

"With me it was sponge toffee in a box in my closet," Tia said as she twisted the fencing pliers, pulled the next section of barbed wire tight, and held it while Sage positioned her staple. "I have a sister who has some serious health problems and has to watch her diet. Her biggest treat was when I'd sneak her some of the forbidden candy."

"I'd eat the licorice at night while I thumbed through magazines." Sage wiped the sweat off her forehead with her sleeve. "My parents made me turn the lights off at ten, so I'd use a flashlight."

"You said they had a lot of lame rules that you didn't like. Was that one of them?" Tia walked through the tall grass to the next post where one of the strands had worked loose. Yanking off her leather gloves, she reached down and picked a bright yellow buffalo bean out of the grass. Pulling the flower apart, she sucked on the tiny drop of nectar inside.

Sage watched her, then did the same. "Hey, it's sweet!" She shredded another flower and tasted the honeyed treat. "My parents had a ton of rules, stupid rules they used to ruin my life."

"Like not letting you look at magazines at night." Tia slipped her gloves back on and twisted the next strand of loose wire with the pliers.

"That and everything else, like what time I had to be in, wanting to know where I was every minute and who I was hanging out with." Sage angrily swung her hammer at the fencing staple and missed, then tried again and missed again.

Tia used her pliers to yank the bent staples out of the post. "Did you ever talk to your parents about how much that bugged you?"

"I did at first and they listened for about a second, then there was a little graffiti incident, and after that, the iron fist came down and I got hammered." Sage pounded the staple home and they moved to the next post. "They never treated me like an adult. The only time I heard anything from them was when I screwed up."

"Have you ever wondered what living with you was like for your parents? Sometimes memory is pretty selective. Maybe you only remember the bad times they yelled and not the good times they didn't." Tia pinned Sage with her gaze, waiting to see if she would understand.

Sage opened her mouth to say something, then closed it. "I'm going to see if Betty wants a drink." She strode away, the thick prairie grass making a *swish, swish, swish* sound against her jeans as she went.

* * *

After supper that night, they returned to their cabin with Tia feeling as though she had made a breakthrough with Sage. Sure, Sage had been angry. In fact, they hadn't spoken much the rest of that afternoon, but Tia knew Sage was thinking about their conversation. She suspected the young runaway had never looked at things from her parents' side before. Tia knew from her classes that lots of times kids simply needed to stop and catch their breath, try to figure things out. She could see how the ranch acted as a buffer zone where kids could do this.

The evening was cool and the setting sun like burnished gold as it streamed through the cabin window. Both Tia and Sage were facing a long evening of work, and neither was looking forward to her gruelling tasks. Tia had decided to do her thousand crunches before tackling her own paper-work and was sweating on her exercise mat.

"This sucks!" Sage complained as she crumpled another sheet of paper. "I hate this junk. I don't see why I have to write a million-page essay about nothing. It's not like the stupid teacher cares about the stuff I write." She'd been struggling with her homework for an hour and the pile of discarded paper was impressive.

Tia's laptop and other items she needed for her work were neatly arranged on the table opposite Sage's cluttered workspace. Sage reached out and flicked Tia's special fuchsia upright stapler with her pen, toppling it over.

"Keep at it. Try again." Tia continued with the workout. "785 … 786 …" Tonight, she had to do her weekly evaluation. Each week the comprehensive report had to be filed with social services, and it was tough to get it right. Tia knew it would take her ages to write, but she had to do a good job. There had been a couple of mistakes in her last report and she didn't want to repeat her errors this week.

When her folks asked her how it was going, she wanted to be able to say she was doing great. She wanted her parents to be proud of her. She wanted her parents to know they could count on her to do the right thing. "787 … 788 …" Spotting the fallen stapler, Tia frowned, jumped up from her mat, and returned it to its upright position before resuming her crunches.

"Jeez, how many of those things are you going to do?" Sage asked, watching Tia as she laboured through the next set.

"Enough to ensure this flabby middle of mine doesn't get any worse," Tia puffed. She saw Sage eye her flat midriff dubiously.

"I'd say from that washboard you've got now that you could give it up for about twenty years and not notice much." Sage went back to her assignment.

Both counsellor and client continued working, the silence punctuated only by Tia's strained counting and Sage's paper crumpling.

Without warning, Sage picked up her notebook and hurled it against the cabin wall. "Forget it! I'm not doing this crap!" She stormed into the bathroom, slamming the door behind her. The picture hanging on the adjoining wall rocked precariously, then slipped off its nail and crashed to the floor. The upright stapler tipped onto its side.

"Great!" Tia wheezed, finishing her thousandth gut-squeezing crunch. "Just great!" She rolled onto her hands and knees and crawled over the scattered pages that were all that remained of Sage's literary effort. Scanning the scribbled notes and scratched-out letters, Tia was vaguely reminded of something she'd seen before.

Before Tia could nail down the thought, the bathroom door opened and a sheepish-looking Sage poked her head out. She saw the splintered shards of glass from the frame lying on the floor. "Sorry." She moved to the pile of broken glass and picked up the pieces.

Tia had studied how rage was often rooted in

frustration. She didn't want to compound the problem by being the resident witch. "I'll get a garbage can. Watch you don't cut your fingers." After righting the stapler, Tia scooped up the pages and stuffed them into a plastic bag, then went in search of the garbage. Sage's green pen was under the table. When Tia picked it up, she saw *The River Club* in gold letters. She was sure it was the one Ty had used the day of the branding.

They were re-hanging the picture, sans glass, when there was a knock at their cabin door and Emma walked in, a plateful of cupcakes in her hands.

"Hi guys! I brought you a late-night snack." She set the plate down on the table. "Looks like you had a little accident." She selected one of the chocolate treats and, flopping down heavily on Tia's bunk, began to eat.

"This was more like collateral damage," Tia said with a sigh.

Tia watched Sage carefully find the cupcake with the least amount of night-flying insects stuck to the icing. "What?" she said defensively when she caught Tia staring. She slouched down in her chair and peeled the paper off her gooey treat.

Tia thought how Sage had been when they were fencing, so happy and talkative, especially when she'd been around Bouncing Betty. Although she was still a little unsure with the horse, Sage had talked as much to Betty as she had to Tia. Here, among people, she was not the same girl.

Emma eyed the remaining treats longingly. "Maybe one more small guy." Giggling self-consciously as she took another, she deftly peeled the wrapper off in one quick movement, then looked at Tia and Sage conspiratorially. "Did you hear about Meagan?" she asked between mouthfuls. "They caught her talking on the cell phone she's been hiding under her mattress. A letter was put in her permanent file. One more screw-up and she goes to juvee to finish her sentence." She gulped the last of her second cupcake. "Have one, Tia. They're chocolate-chip fudge with sprinkles, my favourite. I brought lots." She reached for her third.

"No, thanks." Tia was worried about the waiting report and decided she didn't deserve a reward until the report was done.

"Afraid those iron abs of yours will rust?" Sage piped up.

Tia ignored her and the cupcakes.

"Wow, that's a cool pin." Emma nodded at the dragon brooch Sage had left on the table next to her unfinished assignment.

"It's nothing, an old hunk of junk I found." Sage's tone was nonchalant, but Tia noticed she picked up the brooch and returned it to her pack.

The cabin was cooling off and Tia pulled on her sweatshirt as she said, "I heard the Raise the Roof fund has almost reached its goal. The staff is sure the proceeds from the dance on Saturday night will put it over the top. We'll have a new barn by fall, and the horses will have lots of stalls for cold

January nights." Tia knew everyone had worked hard for a year to raise enough money to finance the massive project, and the dance was the last step. "A lot of specially invited VIPs from Calgary will be attending." She darted a look at Sage. "We can phone and invite family too."

Sage ignored her and looked away.

Emma grinned maliciously, chocolate sprinkles stuck between her teeth like squashed bugs after a motorcycle ride. "Yeah, it sounds like a blast. I wonder if Meagan will be allowed to go?"

The girl was like a mess magnet! Sage had finished her treat and was licking the last morsels of icing off the cupcake paper. As Tia watched, Sage balled the wrapper up and tried unsuccessfully for a corner shot in the overflowing wastepaper basket.

"Sage, we can hang out together at the dance," Emma enthused. "I know exactly what I'll wear. I have a new set of pale blue overalls with a special blouse I've been saving. I might put my hair up; I haven't decided yet. What do you think?"

Tia noticed the note of hero worship in Emma's voice. Apparently, after the barn incident, Sage was the goddess of the day.

"I don't do dances," Sage said indifferently.

"But this one's different. It may be our last chance to talk to people from the outside world until Christmas." Emma sounded petulant. "You could wear your tan cargo pants and I could lend you a navy shirt to accent that beautiful dragon pin. I bet if you crimped your hair…"

"What is this, English as a second language?" Sage interrupted curtly. "I said I *don't* do dances, I *don't* have best friends, and I *don't* like crowd scenes!"

"Sage, maybe you should call your parents and invite them," Tia interjected, hoping to keep things under control. "They would probably like to see where you're staying."

The effect was immediate. Sage turned on Tia like a wild animal. "Look, *Counsellor*," she said harshly, "haven't you noticed, my parents and I don't do the happy family thing. They don't talk to me and I don't talk to them. All our lives work better that way!" She stood up and strode outside, banging the screen door behind her.

"Well, excuse me!" Emma said, rolling her eyes. "I bet she doesn't want to come because she can't dance. She doesn't have to dance, you know. She can sit around the campfire and listen to the guitar playing. Ty said he'd bring his and teach me some chords."

Tia walked to the door and looked out at the indigo sky. The first stars were twinkling like tiny portals into other worlds, mysterious and inviting. As she watched the small silhouette down by the dock, Tia wished Sage could connect with life as easily as she had joined up with old Betty.

"It's almost the witching hour," Emma said as she heaved herself up. "Which for this out-of-control place is ten o'clock. Later." She took her empty plate, leaving behind the ghosts of cupcakes past and the wrapper that Sage had aimed in the general direction of the garbage. Tia picked it up. She still had the dreaded paperwork ahead of her.

A half-hour later, Sage returned with an armload of kindling. Evenings this high in the mountains were chilly, and she busied herself building a fire in the airtight stove. After much cursing and blowing on weakly glowing embers that promptly died out, Sage finally managed to get a decent blaze crackling in the stove. She put the kettle on to heat, then got ready for bed.

Tia stole a glance at her, but didn't say anything as Sage mixed herself a hot chocolate. She finished her preparations and, walking by the table, plunked a mug down in front of Tia.

Skeptically, Tia checked out the cup. Finding it empty, she raised her eyebrows questioningly at Sage.

"You were so worried about your saggy belly, I made you a reduced-calorie, low-fat, no carb, hold-the-foam latte without sprinkles!" She took a long drink from her own mug, leaving a chocolatey moustache on her upper lip before climbing into bed.

* * *

By two-thirty in the morning, Tia still hadn't finished her report and was fighting fatigue as she tried to think straight. Not wanting to disturb

Sage, she worked using only the glow from the wood stove and a small reading light. Bizarre shadows flickered and danced on the cabin walls.

"It's the middle of the night. What are you doing?" Sage's sleepy voice from the top bunk startled Tia and she jumped.

"I'm nearly finished. Go back to sleep." Sage, peering down from her lofty perch like an eagle eyeing a rabbit, watched for a moment, then burrowed back under her covers.

"If you're not careful, you'll be crowned Miss AR of the Circle Four Ranch for Wayward Girls." The sheets muffled Sage's voice.

Tia looked up at the shadowed bed. "And AR means?"

Sage poked her head out of her blanket cocoon. "Miss Anal Retentive!"

Chapter 9

"Are you kidding me? It's six o'clock in the freakin' morning?" Sage groaned and pulled the covers over her head.

"Get up, Sage, you have a snow day from school," Tia encouraged, disregarding the grumbling.

"What are you talking about?" Sage poked her head out from under the blankets, managing to look both sleepy and curious.

Tia pulled on a pair of blue jeans, her hair still wet from her shower. Although she'd worked until two-thirty the night before, she'd been up as usual to get her run in. Despite the high she felt from the run, she was tired now, and the sun had barely crested the horizon.

"I talked to your teacher, and you get the day off from school on the condition that you have your essay done by tomorrow. We're pretty flexible about things like that here." It was true. At the ranch, life lessons were as important as classroom time. Securing a passing grade in the real world was more critical than whether you could do calculus. The repercussions of failure were much more serious.

Tia hurried to the bathroom to pull her hair back into a serviceable ponytail. She inspected her reflection in the mirror. Her chocolate-brown skin shone with health but she looked as tired as she felt, and she wondered if she might get one of those perma-stressed looks she'd seen on some of her professors' faces. "You looked bagged," she told her reflection. "Bedtime early tonight!"

Sage was groggily getting dressed when Tia came back into the main room of the cabin. "Well, if I don't have any school, how come I have to get up before God?" She asked, fighting with a sock.

"You, my dear Sage, are going to help me take a few head of cattle to higher summer pasture, and we need to get an early start. I'll go to the kitchen and pack a lunch; you finish getting ready. I'll meet you down at the barn." She was out the door before Sage could voice any further complaints.

Tia finished saddling Blaster and had just put the bridle on Bouncing Betty when she heard the small side door of the barn open. "I'm back here!" she called, waiting for Sage to drag her butt in.

"Are you going for a morning trail ride?" An unexpected voice asked.

Tia spun around. "Emma! I didn't know you were an early bird." She smiled at the round-faced girl.

"I'm not usually, but I couldn't sleep. And when I noticed Ty's car pull in, I wondered why he was getting back so late." She made a wry face. "Or so early, so I asked him. He said he'd been *detained in the city* and then wanted to know why I was up. That's when I spotted you coming in here, so I told him we were scheduled to go riding this morning, even though we actually weren't, and he must have forgotten."

Tia listened to her long-winded explanation. "Emma, relax! Take a breath!"

The corners of Emma's mouth twitched up. "Right! What it all comes down to is this ... He's going to change his clothes and will be here in five minutes. Can we come?"

Tia knew she should have said no, but it struck her that trail riders weren't supposed to be off the premises all night. She'd been slaving over her computer while Ty was off having fun. If she could go with two hours sleep, it would serve him right to go without any. "We're going to take some cows up to higher pasture and I'd love it if you came along. We can use all the extra hands we can get." She finished saddling Betty. "I'll leave a message with the teacher to spring you from classes. Now, let's get your horses ready to go. Ty's horse is called Satan and, if I remember correctly, you ride Buddy." Together, they had both the horses saddled by the time Ty and Sage finally showed up.

"Sorry I'm late, Tia, my girl." Ty's cheery voice sounded anything but tired as he strode into the barn, and Tia decided there was no way she was going to be the one dragging her butt today. He looked at the waiting horses. "Hey! Thanks for saddling old Satan."

"No worries," Tia said brightly. "If you open the barn door, we can stop by the kitchen and pick up more food. I'm not sure I grabbed enough."

Ty took Satan's reins and opened the big wooden door as Tia gracefully swung into the saddle. She noticed Emma's frown at getting no greeting from Ty, which deepened when he didn't offer to help her onto her horse. Maybe Ty was wisely weaning Emma from her crush.

Sage, who'd been standing quietly in the background, stepped forward. "Betty's monster tall. I can't get on her without help."

Tia knew Sage wasn't a morning person and ignored her whining. "Use the stirrup like I showed you and bounce off your trailing foot."

Sage struggled awkwardly, cursing under her breath, as she clambered aboard Bouncing Betty. "This fleabag won't go where I want!" Sage complained, ineffectually yanking on the reins. "Come on, Betty. Why do you always have to argue with me?" She was hanging on to the saddle horn for dear life as she bobbed up and down and kicked at Betty's ribs to no avail.

"Whoa, Sage! You're about a thousand pounds too light to out-muscle that mare. Go slowly and remember what I told you about soft hands, strong knees," Tia advised.

Tia started forward, knowing Betty would probably follow Blaster. The old mare did and Sage looked triumphant.

"That's better!" Sage said as though she actually had something to do with the direction Betty was going.

* * *

The early morning sun sparkled on the dewy grass, making the world look freshly decorated in diamonds. As the small cattle drive made its way to the high summer pasture, Tia felt content. She liked to herd cattle. Keeping the animals together while they meandered along was a challenge and required sharp eyes, patience and a well-trained horse. Blaster responded instantly to her signals and, together with Ty, they were able to compensate for Sage and Meagan who, though they tried hard, were not very effective.

Throughout the morning, Tia watched Sage closely. She offered advice to improve her riding technique and suggested ways to have Betty do what she wanted with the least amount of effort. Tia could see Sage fighting her own temper and was grateful for the old mare's patience. She nudged Blaster and they cantered up beside the novice rider.

"You look like you were born to ride, Sage. I'm proud of you." Tia saw the young girl straighten in the saddle and even smile a little. She was amazed at what a little praise could do.

"I think it's Betty. She knows what to do with me way more than I know what to do with her." Sage demonstrated her point by trailing the reins across her knees and holding her hands up in the air. Betty continued on, manoeuvring around a boulder in order to keep up with the other horses. "See — look ma, no hands!"

Tia laughed. "It must be your inborn confidence. She feels it from you. Have you always been good with animals? Back home, I mean."

A cloud passed over Sage's face. "I never had any pets when I was at home. They said I wasn't capable of looking after one." She grabbed the reins and forced Betty to go the opposite way around a tree than the one the horse had picked.

"Was it because you had so much trouble at school?" Tia wondered if their previous heart-to-heart had changed Sage's opinion on anything.

"I guess. Also, I was what you might call 'outspoken and independent.' My parents would have said I was 'a mouthy brat who wouldn't listen,' which was probably true." She turned Betty to retrieve a calf that had strayed from his mother.

Tia realized this answer was subtly different from the one she had gotten to her questions the previous day. Sage hadn't immediately condemned her parents for being wrong. "Did you fight with your mom and dad a lot?" With an almost imperceptive signal from Tia, Blaster smoothly intercepted the boisterous calf as it played hide and seek in a clump of willows.

89

Sage struggled as she tried to convince Betty the best way to catch a calf. "I guess you could say I fought a lot and my parents were the targets."

"Do you think you'll ever go home again?" Tia deliberately kept her tone as casual as possible.

"I don't think my parents would be too thrilled about having me around. I was a lot of trouble back then." Sage waggled her coiled rope at the errant calf, which promptly scrambled back to the safety of his mother. "Take that, you little varmint!" she said triumphantly.

"Did you just say *varmint?*" Tia asked, surprised.

Sage spit, barely missing her own boot. "Yup." She grinned at Tia, who found herself smiling back.

They were skirting the edge of the river and the sound of voices made Sage look up. Bobbing down the river were two large rubber rafts, filled with laughing people. The current was strong at this time of year and the boats churned past with great speed. "Hey, where'd they come from?" she asked.

"There's a white-water rafting company around that bend up ahead. This is a Class 4 river — big water and rapids. Tourists drive out and then float downstream to Calgary." Tia watched the boats receding in the distance.

"I've never done anything like that. It looks like fun." Sage continued to stare after the rubber rafts.

90

It did seem like the perfect way to spend a hot summer day. The fast flowing river and the wildly pitching rafts looked like an exciting ride. The riders continued following the riverbank, and when they rounded the bend, a small ferry and several buildings came into sight.

"What's that?" Sage stared at the cable-driven ferry.

"That's where the rafts start out and how they get cars from one side of the river to the other. A car drives onto that barge." Tia pointed at a flat-bottomed boat attached to a thick overhead steel wire. "And the motorized cable drags the ferry across. It cuts the driving time back to Calgary in half."

"So that goat track will take you to the big city?" Sage nodded toward a narrow gravel road on the opposite bank.

"Yes, but don't get any ideas. The ferryman can figure out pretty quickly who belongs and who doesn't. The only habitation around these parts is the ranch, so arriving on horseback is a dead giveaway you're not a tourist."

Tia decided their conversation had been sidetracked long enough. She had been making progress and Sage seemed much more receptive than the last time they'd talked. "You said you were different back then." She didn't know how long a period Sage referred to, but suspected anyone living on the streets would do a lot of growing up fast. "Do you think you've changed?"

Sage took a moment to refocus on what Tia was saying. "Yeah, I guess, but my parents won't know about that."

"They would if you called them, invited them here to the ranch."

Sage's head came up at this. "It wouldn't do any good. My dad got pretty intense when he threw me out. He said I should see what it takes to survive, then maybe I could understand their position more."

"Their position? What's that mean?" Tia was curious.

Sage busied herself adjusting Betty's reins. "I guess they were fed up with me. They racked up a lot in lawyer's fees trying to keep their little girl out of jail for things like oh ..." She looked like she was compiling a list in her head. "Spray painting my zombie of a school teacher's car; stealing a couple of kegs — which sucked because it turned out to be light beer; an arson incident that wasn't my fault, just a wiener roast gone terribly wrong; and a vandalism charge for keying all the guests' cars at our neighbours' lame party."

She didn't look at Tia. "I got tired of listening to their lectures and, well, I'd kind of go nuts and throw things when I got mad, especially when it came to flunking out of school. Once I got carried away and threw a chair through the big front window. After I trashed the house, my dad told me that while I was under his roof, I had to live by his rules. He said if I knew how hard it was to earn a living,

I'd change my attitude. I told him to keep his roof and the stupid rules that went along with it."

"So you packed your bag and headed out to make your fortune." Tia waited for Sage to go on.

"My fortune," she scoffed. "That's a good one. If it weren't for soup kitchens, squeegees, and panhandling, I'd have starved to death." She flapped the reins up and down in an effort to urge Betty forward. "That's another reason I won't call my folks. I bet they'd love to say 'I told you so.'"

Tia wondered about the other Sage Knowles, the one who spray painted a car and threw a chair through her own window. The Sage she knew didn't seem anything like that girl. Tia watched Sage awkwardly moving her horse toward Ty and Emma. "What do you think, old boy?" She rubbed Blaster on the neck. "I doubt her parents would worry about *I told you so*'s if they were given the chance to talk to this Sage Knowles."

Chapter 10

The morning sun warmed the chilly air as the small band of riders continued to move their cattle toward the high alpine meadow. There, the herd would spend the summer growing fat on the lush wild grasses that grew in abundance.

As the terrain became tougher, Tia was glad to see Sage getting a real feel for her horse. By the time they started the steep climb to the summer pastureland, Sage was doing well, despite her complaints.

"I have to rest again, Tia. My butt has gone numb." Sage trotted up to her trail rider, trying not to look like the greenhorn she was.

"Sage, you're doing such a great job, you deserve a break. I'm impressed with the way you handle Betty." Tia's praise was honest and Sage responded with a pretty blush. She dipped her head so that her hair hid her face, and Tia couldn't see if she was smiling or not. She suspected Sage was not used to open praise and decided everyone needed warm fuzzies, including Sage Knowles, veteran hard case.

"We're thinking of stopping for lunch. What do you think?" Tia called back to Ty and Emma, who brought up the rear of their mini-cattledrive.

"Sounds good," Ty said as he took off his hat and wiped his brow. "Man, I hope you brought coffee."

Tia heard the fatigue in his voice and had to admit she could use some. "I need a caffeine IV."

They headed for a field by a small stream. The cattle were content to slurp water from the creek and graze on the thick green grass.

Emma waited for Ty to help her down, but instead he walked over to Tia and took her reins before he tied both their horses up. Emma's face turned as dark as a thundercloud, and Tia wondered if this was part of Ty's keeping Emma at a distance. She'd noticed that Ty could be very friendly with his client, then at other times he was deliberately cool. She decided that, since he did have more experience than she did with troubled teens, he must know what he was doing.

Sage pulled the sandwiches out of the saddlebags and checked each one. "Good effort on the gourmet lunch, Tia. Peanut butter and jelly is always the first choice of any fine dining establishment."

Her tone was light and playful, and the lack of

bitterness was new. Tia had been wondering if she'd made a mistake with the sandwiches. Perhaps she should have made something more substantial. As she watched the way Sage demolished the simple fare, she was reassured. It may not be fancy, but it was going down fine all the same.

Having dismounted on her own, Emma joined them. "One sandwich or two, Emma?" Tia asked. "I made lots — but be warned, they're plain old PB and J."

Emma's face lit up. "Can I have three? I'm starving to death."

Tia shot Sage a look of triumph at Emma's enthusiasm for the "plain old PB and J." "The drinks are in Ty's saddle bags. I'll get you one." She walked over to Satan and rummaged for the sodas. Ty had stuffed his jacket into the saddlebags, and as Tia pulled it out, a letter fell from the pocket and fluttered to the ground. She stooped to pick it up, noticing the letterhead was that of a law firm in Denver, Colorado. The first line caught her eye. *The case brought by the Denver Way Station for Girls against Shelly Gonzalez for theft over $2000.00 has resulted in a guilty verdict.* Tia read on, unable to stop herself. The young girl had been remanded to a Young Offenders Centre for a period of two years.

"Shelly was a bad one with a record for car theft, and there was corroborating evidence regarding the money." Ty's voice startled Tia. She turned to find him right behind her. "She would have been convicted without my testimony. It's a sad case. I had high hopes for the girl and had tried to help her, but …" He shook his head and sighed. "You can't win them all."

Tia looked into his face. "I'm sorry, Ty." She handed him the letter.

"I received that yesterday and went to talk to a lawyer friend of mine to see if we could do something to get her a lighter sentence. That's why I was out last night. Two years to a sixteen-year-old is like a life sentence, but there was nothing we could do." He stuffed the letter back into his pack.

Tia saw the slump of his shoulders and felt terrible. It had been a great day up until now. Watching Ty walk away, Tia realized the career she had chosen was not going to be an easy one. She gave Emma her drink, then refilled the coffee mug and joined Ty by the creek.

Sage wandered off to skip stones across the rippling stream as the two trail riders sipped their steaming brew.

"It's so beautiful up here, I'd have taken this job without pay," Tia said with a sigh.

Ty leaned back against the sun-warmed grass. "Not me. I'm always happiest on payday. There's always too much week left at the end of my cheque," he joked. "If it took a nickel to go around the world, I couldn't get out of sight."

Tia laughed, glad to see Ty back in high spirits. She thought of her own cheque. There wasn't anywhere to spend money on the ranch, and by the end of the summer, she'd have quite a sum saved. Her parents would be delighted when she told them she would pay her own tuition for the next year of university. It was, after all, the responsible thing to do.

After finishing lunch, the four riders remounted and started the last push to the grazing lease. The cattle, sensing freedom, had begun to get frisky, or at least as frisky as animals that size could get.

Finally, the riders cleared the last rise and Tia saw the boundary fence to the lease. "There's a Texas gate. The cows won't be able to get through. We'll have to follow the fence line until we find one they can cross." Tia and Blaster started looking for a barbed wire gate. She knew there'd be an opening eventually and hoped she'd picked the right direction. Then she spotted what she was looking for. "It's in the next gully!" she shouted over her shoulder.

Ty drove the herd after Tia, slapping his rope on his jeans and whistling loudly to keep the cattle moving. Two young steers split off and disappeared into the brush.

Tia knew they had to be rounded up quickly before they were completely lost. "Sage! Get the stragglers. I'll help Ty with the rest!" Sage started after them. "Emma, give Sage a hand!" Tia knew it was impossible for one rider to control two animals that didn't want to co-operate. Emma started after Sage.

Tia climbed off her horse and opened the barbed wire gate, dragging it to one side as Ty deftly moved the cattle through. When the last bellowing cow had ambled after her friends, Tia secured the crude gate. "Job done, except for the two the girls are chasing!"

A high-pitched scream echoed through the valley.

The hairs on the back of Tia's neck stood up. Adrenaline pumped into her system as she ran for Blaster. Within seconds, she was back in her saddle and galloping after Sage and Emma.

Chapter 11

Tia came over the rise and looked down at a scene that made her blood run cold. In the small alpine valley, Sage stood face to face with a huge black bear.

Obviously frightened, Bouncing Betty was behind Sage. Emma had been thrown and was lying on the ground writhing in pain as she held on to the reins of her own terrified animal.

"Oh, God!" Tia whispered, then slapped Blaster on the flanks and started down the steep slope, slipping and sliding on the loose scree.

Blaster pulled up short when they reached the bottom, the scent of the bear making his nostrils flare. Tia knew not to force him. She would only end up fighting to control an animal whose natural instinct told it to run for its life.

Jumping off her horse, Tia tied him to a tree, then pulled a slim silver rod the size of an oversized pen out of her sleeve pocket.

"Don't move!" Tia whispered as she moved quietly toward Sage. She hoped the inexperienced teen wouldn't provoke the bear into an attack. Tia edged as close as she dared, then held the silver tube in both hands, pointed it toward the sky, and depressed a button on the side.

A round plastic cartridge fired out of the pen and streaked skyward. It arced upward, then hung for a second before exploding in the air above the bear with a very loud *bang*.

The bear jerked at the noise. With a roar of outrage, the large animal rose onto two feet, pawed at the air, then dropped down onto all fours and bolted into the bush. The speed with which it moved amazed Tia. There was no way anyone could outrun a bear.

This was too much for Betty, who gave the horse equivalent of a scream, jerked the reins out of Sage's hands, and fled to the far side of the field.

"Are you all right, Sage?" Tia asked anxiously as she hurried over.

Sage nodded, her eyes never leaving the spot where the bear had disappeared. Pale faced, she flicked a questioning glance at the device in Tia's hand before her eyes went back to scanning the bush.

"Bear Banger," Tia explained as she tucked the handy device into her sleeve pocket. "Don't leave home without it." She turned to Emma.

Ty, who had been behind Tia, was now trying to

control Buddy, but the noise from the Bear Banger had sent the already frightened horse into a frenzy.

"Get Emma out of here!" he yelled as he struggled with the crazed horse.

Dodging the flailing hooves, Tia dragged the whimpering girl away. She noticed a half eaten jar of peanut butter lying on the ground beside her.

"My ankle," Emma moaned, her face contorted with pain. "It hurts."

Tia looked at the ankle, which was already swelling. "Can you move your toes?"

Emma winced, then nodded.

"I think it's sprained. I've got a tensor bandage in my saddlebags." Tia retrieved the first-aid supplies and gently worked Emma's boot off her foot.

Sage, who had remained staring after the bear, now scrambled over, her face chalk white. "What are you doing? We've got to go! It could come back!"

"What we have to do is keep our heads," Tia said calmly. "We have to look after Emma."

"Leave her! If she hadn't been stuffing her fat face with peanut butter, the bear wouldn't have smelled it and come for snacks!" Sage said excitedly.

"Drop dead!" Emma yelled, grimacing as she kicked out at Sage with her good leg.

"That's enough, both of you." Tia snapped. "We're not going anywhere until I look after this ankle." She gently wrapped the injured leg.

Sage turned and frantically scanned the bushes for the bear.

Ty had calmed Buddy enough to walk him over to Tia. He'd also retrieved Bouncing Betty, who was tossing her head nervously. "Satan's tied up over the rise. Blaster doesn't seem too worried." He nodded toward Tia's stallion that was, while keeping a wary eye out to his surroundings, waiting patiently. "You take the girls and head back to the ranch while I find the strays that got us into this fix in the first place." Ty looked around for the missing steers. "They won't have gone far. I'll put them in with the rest and catch up."

"Can you ride?" Tia asked Emma as she finished wrapping the ankle.

"I think so. Will you help me onto my horse, Ty?" Emma smiled up expectantly at her hero.

"In a minute." Ty moved beside Sage, leaving Emma fuming impatiently. "You were very brave with that bear," he said admiringly. "I don't want to think of what might have happened if you'd run." He handed Sage the reins to her horse. "Hold tight to this old girl. I don't want to be chasing her again."

Sage still looked wild-eyed to Tia, but she accepted Betty's reins without question.

Ty turned back to his injured client. "Okay, Emma, my girl. I bet I can have you back on Buddy in three minutes or less." He handed Tia the reins. "You hold him still while I help Emma."

Smiling, Emma blinked back tears as she held her arms up to Ty. "I'll need a little help to stand." Her voice sounded whispery and weak.

Sage continued to look around nervously and Tia saw that she was genuinely frightened. For all her tough talk, Sage was as vulnerable as anyone when confronted with a terrifying situation. "Don't worry. That bear is probably in British Columbia by now," Tia said reassuringly.

"But it could double back." Sage's voice was filled with panic. "We have to go — now!" She pulled on Betty's reins, trying to force the horse to move closer so she could mount. Betty whinnied and pulled her head back, nearly dragging Sage off her feet. Mouth set in a determined line, Sage responded by yanking harder.

"Stop it, Sage! You're freaking Betty out. She's scared too." Tia had her hands full keeping Buddy steady.

Sage again tried to bully the horse into submission, but Betty resisted, terrified. Tia could see the situation was nearly out of control. Sage's own fear was being communicated to the horse. The terror in Sage's eyes made Tia realize how close to the edge she was.

She understood Sage's fear. This was a city girl, new to fresh air and forests, not to mention cows and horses. On her first trail ride she'd been confronted with a walking meat grinder! She had little control of her horse, less of her surroundings, and none of the bear. Her life must seem like a roller-coaster ride with no one at the controls.

Guilt hit Tia like a physical blow. She should have gone with Sage to collect those strays instead of staying with Ty. Sage was a greenhorn and Emma wasn't much better. She could have stopped Sage from wandering into the path of that bear and Emma wouldn't be lying on the ground in pain. As far as her performance as a counsellor went, she deserved an F.

Using her soft horse-training voice, Tia tried to get Sage to forget her own fears and focus on helping her horse. "Betty is very frightened, Sage. Talk to her. She trusts you. She needs you to be the strong one, to lead her away from here, away from the danger. Sage, remember what we did in the barn. Talk to her, use the join-up technique." Tia hoped her words would get through.

Suddenly, Sage stopped yanking at the panicked animal, and then her brain seemed to click. She made low murmuring sounds to the horse, avoided eye contact, and turned her body at an angle to the animal. The effect was immediate. Both horse and girl calmed down. Sage gently led Betty around, the reins over her shoulder as they walked in a circle.

"That's it. Now, keep talking to her," Tia encouraged as she continued to hold Buddy steady.

Sage spoke in a soothing voice. "Don't worry, girl, that bear's history. It's going to be okay. I know you wanted to stay with me, but you were scared. You thought you'd die if you didn't get out of there." The horse's ears flicked forward, listening. Sage continued talking to the frightened animal. "I won't let anything happen to you. I'll fight for you and will never desert you even if a hundred bears come for supper. That's what real friends do. When we get home, I'll rub you down and give you extra oats." Betty snorted and moved up closer, then laid her head on Sage's shoulder. Sage reached up and rubbed the horse's nose as they continued walking.

Tia was astonished. It was working. Sage was so focused on helping Betty, her own fear was gone. Tia turned her attention back to Emma and Ty. Ty was trying to help Emma into the saddle but without the use of one of Emma's legs, it was a struggle. Emma looked uncomfortable as Ty pushed and lifted until she was finally able to swing her leg over the horse and pull herself up.

"Phew! Are you going to be able to stay there okay?" He asked, wiping the back of his neck with his kerchief.

Emma adjusted herself, then smiled down at him as though he was a knight in shining armour. "Of course. Ty, thanks for the help with Buddy. The way he was putting the boots to everything, I could have been killed."

Tia couldn't believe what she was hearing. Hadn't she noticed that it was Tia who had driven off the bear? Talk about love being blind! She swung up onto Blaster, looking around for Sage.

Sage had stopped walking and was quietly stroking Betty's broad nose. Tia smiled to herself. Sage was now in control, and not just of the horse.

When they finally arrived back at the ranch, all four were exhausted. Sage went to stable the horses while the doctor looked after Emma in the infirmary.

"Don't worry, the doc agrees it's sprained not broken." Ty helped Emma with her new crutches. "You'll be fine in no time."

"I'm afraid I'm no good at these things." Emma waved one of the crutches, lost her balance, and almost fell over.

"Hey! That's not what we want!" Ty reached out to steady the girl.

"I guess I'll need help back to my cabin." Emma slumped on her crutches as though she weren't sure she could stand with them, let alone get all the way back to her cabin.

"No problem," Ty volunteered.

Tia, who'd waited to hear what the doctor said, decided Emma didn't give up easily when she wanted something, and from the way she acted around Ty, he was number one on her wish list. "I'm going to the barn." She started out of the infirmary. "Don't worry about your horse, Emma. Sage and I can look after Buddy for you."

The light was on in the barn when Tia walked in. It was quiet and she could hear Sage in conversation with someone. Tia noticed with surprise that all their horses had been put in box stalls, rubbed down, and fed. Sage had been busy. As she got closer to Betty's stall, she stopped. Sage was brushing her horse and talking.

"Don't worry, I won't leave you. You're so much prettier than that nag of Emma's, and so much braver!" She put her brush down and took her small camera out, snapping a shot of the horse. "There, digitally perfect. Do you want to see?" She showed the horse the tiny screen. "You look good. Except for that one little lapse, you hardly spooked at all today. I thought it was going to get ugly when that fleabag Buddy tried to flatten Emma. Did I mention you're much smarter than Buddy, too?" Sage kissed Betty on the muzzle. "And you smell way better," she giggled, "than Emma, I mean!"

Tia smiled. Sage had made a friend; she'd connected with the horse.

This was the first real chink in the angry girl's armour, and it gave Tia hope.

Chapter 12

The night of the Raise the Roof dance was clear and starry with a hint of smoke drifting on the breeze. Twinkling lights were strung around the ranch and music played over loudspeakers. Everywhere there was a festive air.

"Man, can you believe this great turnout!" Tia, standing in the food line, took the plate she was handed. "With a crowd this size, it's sure to put the building fund over the top." Ty waited next to her, but seemed distracted. "Ty, the money for the barn …"

"What? Oh sorry, Tia. I think you're *right on the money*." He smiled apologetically at his lame joke. "I was at the admin building earlier and everyone's betting the cash brought in tonight will buy us the deluxe package. Sara's already picking out extras we hadn't even thought about because the money's been so tight. Lots of high rollers turned out, and they don't seem to have any trouble opening their wallets for a good cause."

Tia noticed Ty carried two plates of food when he followed her back to the campfire. "You stocking up for winter?" She asked good-naturedly.

"No, one's for Emma. Poor kid can't walk without help, so I said I'd bring her some food."

At the campfire Sage, Meagan, and Sara were sitting and eating, their faces glowing in the firelight. Tia had talked to Sara and suggested the girls get together for supper as a way to get them to talk and perhaps resolve their differences.

Emma, her crutches propped on a boulder, looked like a kid on the wrong side of a candy store window as she watched the others enjoy their meals.

As Ty walked up, Meagan eyed the two heaping plates. "Emma said you were getting the food, but I see you only brought enough for her."

"Shut up, Meagan!" Emma shot back.

"Ty doesn't want her to waste away to nothing," Sage added without looking up from her own plate.

Tia knew Sage still blamed the bear attack on Emma and her peanut butter snack.

"I wouldn't want to be a walking stick-figure like you, Sage!" Emma retorted. "I'm surprised you lasted as long as you did on the street. I heard no John would pay for your bony ass."

"I never offered it! Besides, you were giving it away so cheap you had the market cornered," Sage said derisively.

As Tia listened, she hoped what Sage had said was true and she'd never resorted to selling herself to survive. She knew most girls on the street did.

Emma took the plate offered. "Thanks, Ty. Sit by me. I saved you a spot." She smiled and indicated the camp chair next to her, patting it with her hand.

"Jeez, Ty, it sucks to be you!" Sage scoffed as he took the seat.

Tia noticed Emma had on a lot of makeup; her bright orange lipstick practically glowed in the firelight. The new tan overalls she wore were fine, but the "special blouse" was verging on X-rated! The off-the-shoulder white peasant blouse was very low-cut and exposed way too much for a casual night around a campfire.

Tia wore a new blue denim skirt and embroidered vest with a soft pink checked blouse, which looked good with her dark skin. She'd encouraged Sage to dress up for the evening's events and mentioned the outfit Emma had suggested, but Sage had flatly refused. She'd said the only reason she was going was for the food.

As though right on cue, Emma zeroed in on Sage's fashion failure.

"Gee, you really put a lot of effort into your outfit, Sage," Emma commented sarcastically. "You could have at least worn that cool pin."

"What pin?" Sara asked conversationally.

"Sage has a gold brooch shaped like a dragon

and it would have looked nice with the outfit I suggested she wear tonight. But," Emma sniffed, "she didn't take my advice."

"Smart girl. Not everyone wants to look like a bargain-basement hooker." Meagan bit into her hamburger. "People are talking about what a freaking hero you are, Sage. You saved the bear from eating a high-fat meal!" She glanced pointedly at Emma and laughed.

"You're about as funny as a pay toilet in a diarrhea ward," Emma sneered.

"I wouldn't talk, Miss Piggy," Meagan snapped. "And if you think Sage will be your best buddy now, I've got news for you. Miss Congeniality was only saving her own butt and she would have tossed your sorry ass to the bear if she could have lifted it."

"Meagan, settle down," Sara interrupted. "I'd like to hear Sage's story myself. Sage why don't you tell us what happened?"

Tia knew Sara was trying to draw out the reticent teen by having her talk about the incident, but she also knew that psych games wouldn't work. Sage was too smart to fall for them.

Sage threw her empty paper plate into the fire, then dusted off her hands. "Damn straight, Meagan. I was looking out for number one and would have done the same if it had been you."

So much for getting Sage to talk, Tia thought. The score was Sage 1, Sara 0.

Meagan tossed a piece of her hotdog bun at

Sage, hitting her hair, where the mustard stuck. Before Tia could react, Sage shot across the space between them and shoved Meagan off the rock she'd been perched on and into the dirt. Meagan wore an extremely short, tight black leather skirt that ended up threatening to become a belt.

"Sage, that's enough!" Tia said loudly. All three counsellors reacted by jumping between the two girls before the situation escalated to more serious blows.

"You'll pay for that, you freakin' creep!" Meagan hissed through clenched teeth, as she picked herself up and tugged her skirt back down over her bare thighs.

Ignoring her, Sage calmly took her camera out and looked through the viewfinder as she went back to her seat. The score was now Sage 2, the rest of the world 0.

"Meagan, sit down," Ty said firmly, "and let me eat in peace."

"Has anyone noticed the smell of smoke in the air?" Sara asked, diverting the conversation as everyone resumed eating their meals. The tension around the fire eased.

"I did." Tia recalled the acrid smell she'd noticed earlier. "Is it something we should be worried about?" She positioned herself between Sage and Meagan.

"It's a forest fire in the next valley. Alberta Fish and Wildlife says it's under control, and unless something happens, like a wind shift, it's no big deal." Sara popped the last bite of her steak into her mouth. "Mmm, that was good. I think I have enough room for dessert. You up for some fresh rhubarb pie, Meagan?"

"Anything to get away from here." Meagan stood. "Oh, and Sage — I'd watch my back if I were you. Emma here is not big on loyalty. She's been known to throw a few friends to the bears herself."

"As if," Emma sniffed, but Tia remembered the incident with the cellphone.

"What a glorious night!" Ty leaned back against his camp chair and studied the sky. "All that's missing is a chilled glass of Chardonnay." Looking over at Tia, he smiled lazily as he picked up his guitar. "Hey, once the kids are in bed, I'll grab a bottle from my private wine cellar and we can relax under the stars."

His dark eyes had a new look in them, one that made Tia feel warm all over. She wasn't sure he was kidding about the wine. With Ty, she never knew. "I'm trying to cut down," she laughed nervously.

"I like a nice Merlot," Emma interjected.

"Maybe in a couple of years, Emma, my girl." Ty smiled.

Emma sat up straight and thrust out her ample chest. "I'm not a girl, I'm a woman!"

"My apologies! Most ladies don't like to get older any faster than they have to." Ty strummed his guitar and Tia wondered if his quirky sense of humour would get him into trouble one day.

Sage abruptly stood up. "This bites. I'm going to check on Betty."

* * *

They spent the next hour singing campfire songs as Ty played requests. He was good and a lot of people drifted over, drawn by the music. Before long, it had turned into an old-fashioned sing-along.

As the evening wore on, Tia began to get edgy about not finishing her paperwork. She'd been working on her Weekly Report and it still wasn't done. She tried to enjoy the music, but the feeling persisted. She checked the time.

"What's the matter? Late for a hot date?" Ty asked between songs. "That's the fourth time you've looked at your watch."

Tia shook her head. "No such luck. Look, Ty, I have to do something at my cabin. If I stop at the barn and send Sage back, could you watch her for me? I won't be long."

Ty strummed a chord on his guitar. "No problem. I like a big audience. Hurry back, I'll save you a special seat." He pulled the chair next to him a little closer.

Tia went to the barn, but Sage wasn't there. She knew she should find her, but she had to get to her report. Sage was probably busy taking incriminating pictures with that camera of hers. Sure her client would wander back to the campfire eventually, Tia hurried to the cabin. She'd finish up, then zip back to join the sing-along before she was even missed.

* * *

Tia had been working for a while when the screen door squeaked open and Sage ambled in. "Hi. Do you want to come back to the lame ho-down with me? Your boyfriend is going to give us a yodelling show."

Tia was right in the middle of a crucial point. "Ah, no. You go ahead and I'll catch up." She frowned at the computer screen.

"I thought we could build some of those *S'mores* things. I've never made any before and Emma says they're great, which probably means your hips will never recover. But if you're game, so am I."

"Damn it!" Tia had hit the wrong keys and had to retype her last two sentences. "I said not now, Sage." She glanced at her watch. It was nearly eleven. "I'm almost done. Let me finish this and I'll catch up."

The screen door closed as Tia completed the critical paragraph. The jargon she used was tricky and she hoped the report didn't sound like a rookie had written it.

Twenty minutes later, the screen door creaked again and Ty poked his head in. "How about that drink?" he asked with a mischievous grin.

Tia knew this was taking longer than expected, but she simply had to finish. "I'm nearly done and I could use a hot chocolate. Give me ten minutes and I'll meet you at the campfire." She dismissed him with an apologetic smile.

Tia checked and rechecked her spelling and grammar until it was perfect. When she looked at her watch, she was shocked to see it was nearly 1.00 A.M.! *Oh no! Where was Sage?* She should have checked on her hours ago. Grabbing a sweater, Tia sprinted out of the cabin.

The party was to end at midnight, and when Tia returned to the campfire it was deserted, with only glowing embers left in the stone firepit. Ty's guitar leaned against a rock. Without the crackling flames, the whole area seemed dark and forlorn. Looking up at the sky, Tia noticed that the stars were no longer visible and the smell of smoke was much stronger than it had been earlier.

Tia knew Sage loved to spend every spare minute in the barn with Betty, and hoped this was where she was now. She hurried into the warm earthy-smelling building and heard Sage mumbling to her horse.

Sighing with relief, Tia walked to Betty's stall, then stopped. "Oh, my God!"

Sage was slouched against the wooden stall, straw stuck in her tousled hair and lying beside her were two empty wine bottles.

She was totally out-of-her-mind drunk!

Chapter 13

"What were you thinking last night?" Tia's temper was barely under control as she yanked her clothes on after her shower. She was furious with Sage, which made it hard to behave like a professional counsellor. A sinking feeling told her that her client may be one of those Ty had mentioned, the ones who were basically lost causes and a waste of energy.

Leaving the girl sleeping, Tia had gone for her morning run and hoped she'd come to a decision on what to do by the time she came back. If she reported Sage as she was supposed to, there would be an investigation. When asked if her client had contravened any other rules, Tia would have to admit to the incident in the barn with the branding iron, the stolen cigarettes, and last night's attack on Meagan. It wouldn't go well for Sage or, Tia realized, for herself. "I need an answer now, and it had better be a good one."

Sage grimaced and pulled the pillow over her head. "Jeez, stop shouting, will you?"

Tia stormed over and snatched the pillow away. "I asked you what happened." Her voice was strained and she really wanted to smack Sage with the pillow. Instead, she tossed the potential weapon safely into the corner.

Sage put a thin arm across her eyes. "I was taking pictures of all the geeks wandering around and ended up near the admin building. I remembered your boyfriend had joked that he had a booze stash and, since I already knew where his hidey-hole was, I decided to check it out. He wasn't kidding." She winced. "Since you'd blown me off, I decided to amuse myself and got totally wasted."

Tia flinched. True, she had ignored Sage, but that didn't give the teen the right to break into the admin building, steal liquor, and get drunk! "You're right, I screwed up. I apologize. I shouldn't have ditched you." She returned the conversation to the proper track. "Then what happened?"

Sage belched loudly, her breath sour. "When it comes to who I choose to spend my time with, old Betty wins hands-down. You can trust a horse like nobody's business and that girl knows how to keep a secret." Sage scratched in a very unladylike way. "I took two bottles to the barn and partied with her. Mine went down pretty quickly and, since Betty's on the wagon, I drank hers too." She pitched a bleary eye at Tia. "Any idea what happened to those dead soldiers? The narcs would have a fit if they found them."

Tia felt her face flush hotly. Before half carrying Sage back to the cabin, she had hidden the evidence in the bottom of the garbage bin. Thinking about it, that had probably made things worse. It looked like she was covering up for Sage, but she had needed time to figure out what to do.

Tia ignored Sage's strange humour and didn't answer her question. "We've both seriously screwed up, Sage. You feed the horses. I have to go to the administration building. Apparently, they want to talk to me. Any guesses about what?" Pulling her hoodie on, Tia stomped out of the cabin and slammed the door.

* * *

Dr. John Stone, the chief administrator, looked grim as he called everyone into the conference room.

"What's this about?" Tia whispered, sliding into the seat next to Ty. Since everyone had been called to the meeting, she didn't think it was about Sage. This gave her a little more time to decide what to do.

"I haven't a clue. After the get-together around the campfire, I took Emma back to her cabin and everything was fine. What happened to you?" Ty gave her a sidelong glance. "I thought we were going to get together for a nightcap?"

Tia felt a little uncomfortable. He must not

know that Sage had beaten him to his stash. "To tell you the truth, I didn't think you were serious and … ah, it took longer than I thought to finish that stuff I was working on. Can I have a rain check?"

He squeezed her hand, holding on a second longer than he had to. "For you, anytime."

His touch was warm and strangely comforting. Tia felt his strength and wished she were as strong and confident. Sage's complete disregard for the rules and, for that matter, for Tia had shaken her. Maybe this wasn't what she was cut out for. Maybe she'd chosen the wrong career. So far, she hadn't done much right when it came to saving Sage Knowles from Sage Knowles!

"I have some unfortunate news, everyone," Dr. Stone interrupted. "Sometime after eleven o'clock last night, the money from the Raise the Roof Dance, including some very generous corporate donations, as well as staff cash, was stolen from the administration building."

There was an immediate buzz of conversation around the room.

"Quiet, please!" He held his hand up for silence. "I can't give you the exact amount, but it was over ten thousand dollars. The RCMP are on their way. Each of you will have to account for your client's whereabouts last night. I'm sure this won't be difficult. It's purely a formality."

Tia felt like all the air had been sucked out of the room.

"Are you all right?" Ty asked. "You look a little green around the gills."

"I … I need some air. I haven't had breakfast and feel light-headed from my run." Tia was about to excuse herself when Dr. Stone spoke up again.

"One more bad piece of news, people." He ran his hand through his wavy white hair. "The fire that was under control in the next valley has taken a serious turn for the worse. The forest service is watching the situation closely, but we've been put on evacuation alert in case the wind shifts. Make sure everyone is ready to leave quickly. I have extra vans and horse trailers on standby in case we have to clear out in a hurry. I'll keep you posted."

Tia stood, speechless. She couldn't believe the news about the theft.

"All that money. This is incredible." Ty's face showed his astonishment. "I know there were a lot of strangers here last night, but whoever did this would have to know their way around the admin building and where the money was locked up. It sounds like an inside job." He looked to where Dr. Stone stood with several trail riders. "I'll talk to John. Maybe he's not telling us everything."

Tia couldn't breath. "I'll wait outside." She pushed her way through the tangle of staff and out onto the veranda. Her mind swirled with a million thoughts, all of them dismal. She knew she was in serious trouble for ignoring her client last night, but worse than that, had Sage committed a major crime? Tia wasn't sure that being drunk in a barn with your best friend, who happened to be a horse, was an alibi or an admission of guilt.

Grim faced, Ty came through the door. "It's bad news." He took Tia's hand she fought the warm feeling the gesture gave her. "What John didn't make public was that they found a piece of evidence in the bushes beside the building. They think the thief dropped it during the robbery."

Tia's throat tightened. "What did they find?"

"It was an expensive gold brooch shaped like ..." His voice trailed off.

"... a dragon," she finished dejectedly as her stomach lurched.

Ty nodded. "I'm sorry, Tia. I hope you can vouch for Sage's whereabouts last night, because when the police get here, they're going to ask some hard questions about your client."

Tia couldn't look him in the eye. "Ah, Sage was in the barn until very late." True, but it was the part she didn't tell Ty that had her stomach twisted into knots. She felt nauseous. "I have to go." Hastily, she dropped Ty's hand, then brushed past the tall trail rider. She had to know exactly what Sage had done last night, how she got into the admin building, and what time she partied with Betty. Once the details of Sage's time at the ranch came out, combined with incriminating evidence found at the scene and her past record of theft ... even to Tia it looked like an open and shut case.

Guilt washed over her. She had let Sage down seriously last night. If she hadn't stayed to finish that stupid report and had instead gone to the sing-along, none of this would be an issue. Some counsellor she was!

As Tia hurried toward the barn, she prayed Sage hadn't helped herself to more than the wine on her midnight raid. She wondered again if she'd been wrong about the young runaway. Had Sage completely fooled her into thinking she was re-evaluating her life, turning things around? Was she, after all, one of those lost girls that Ty had warned her about? She heard Sage talking as she entered the barn.

"I'm telling you, Blaster, you missed a wicked blowout last night. It really rocked!" Sage was in the stall next to Blaster's, brushing Betty. The old mare nickered softly as if agreeing with her new best friend.

"We've got to talk." Sage looked up as Tia barged into the stall.

"What's the matter? Am I going to be banished to a place worse than this?" Sage tossed the comment casually, but Tia heard an echo of worry.

"Actually, you weren't the main focus of the discussion." Tia wondered if this was the truth. There was a real possibility that Dr. Stone had, in fact, been talking about Sage when he was speaking of the thief. "At least, I hope not."

Sage rubbed her forehead. "I've got a real pounder, and don't want to play games. You're obviously cranked about something. So what happened?"

Tia crossed her arms. "Last night, right around the time you say you took the wine, someone stole a large amount of money from the admin building."

Sage's eye's grew round as she made the leap to the obvious conclusion. "So naturally you think it was me! That's totally bogus." She tossed the brush she'd been using into the small tack box she'd set up exclusively for her implements for Betty. "I supposed you narked on me about the booze?" Her eyes flashed with a combinations of guilt and defiance.

"No, I didn't say a word to anyone about you being in the building last night or any night." Tia wasn't sure how to tell her about the pin. "They found a clue as to who stole the money."

"Good, I hope they catch the freak." Sage looked relieved.

Tia licked her lips, then dropped her bombshell. "Actually, the clue they found was a piece of jewellery, a very distinctive gold brooch shaped like a dragon."

Sage's eyes flew wide open. "What? My pin? Are you wack? I didn't take that money."

"But you were there. You took the wine."

"Yeah, so? Big diff between boosting a couple of bottles and ripping off the ranch for a bagload of cash." Sage paced agitatedly around the stall, making Betty's ears prick forward uneasily as she sensed Sage's distress.

"What about your fingerprints? They'll be all

over the office. And I'm sure the forensic people can tell the door was jimmied, even though you thoughtfully locked up after yourself." Tia was trying to think like a cop and it added up to one thing — Sage Knowles was the thief.

"A lot of people's fingerprints will be in the office." Sage looked at her pointedly. "And not all of them legal. I'm not the only one who's been in there. That door has been busted so many times, it's a joke."

Tia thought about the cigarettes. "Did anyone see you going into or coming out of the building?"

"I don't know," Sage snapped. "It doesn't matter anyway. They have my pin, which puts me at centre stage. As my trail rider, they'll ask you where I was and you'll have to tell them I was in the barn hammered out of my mind. Next question will be where did I get the booze, and you say the admin building. Bingo! Game over for me."

"Sage, you probably figured out that I don't have a lot of experience as a counsellor…"

"No kidding, Sherlock," Sage scoffed.

Tia had had enough. "Drop the attitude, it's not helping," she said curtly, then pressed on. "I've seen enough *Law and Order* on TV to know you are going to be the prime suspect. It adds up to an open-and-shut case."

"Tia, you have to believe me. I didn't take the money." Sage looked her straight in the eyes. "Honest. I swear on Betty's life."

Something in the way her voice caught made

Tia stop. "I don't know what to believe," she said tiredly.

"Okay, okay ..." Sage was desperate. "Think about this. You've been around me enough to know I'm too smart to risk being caught stealing on a night when there were so many people hanging out. That would be dumb when I could break in any time I wanted. And why would I steal the money and then get drunk? Why do a big crime and then take the risk of getting caught for a small one? You saw me — I could hardly stand, let alone mastermind a break-in. And why would I go back to our cabin, get a pin that everyone knows is mine, and then be so stupid as to lose it in the bushes? Tia, this is a frame."

What Sage said made sense. Tia looked at her closely. If she was acting, she deserved an Academy Award. She looked scared and sounded innocent. Then Tia thought about her client's less than stellar record at the ranch, and the things Sage had confided to her that she'd done in the past. "Sage, I need to think about all this."

"*I didn't do it!*" Sage's voice cracked.

Tia saw her client's tear-bright eyes and she wanted to believe her. But what Sage had said was right — Sage was not stupid. She was, in fact, very smart. Was she clever enough to plant evidence against herself, then get drunk so it would look like she was framed? Could she be that devious? Tia hated the idea that she was being conned, but if she wasn't, she owed it to Sage to find out the truth. "Guilty or innocent, we're going to get to the bottom of this. I promise."

Sage blinked back the tears that were threatening to ruin her tough punk image, and Tia felt her verdict shifting to the innocent side. "Now, first things first. How did that pin end up in the bushes? When was the last time you saw it?"

"I always keep it stashed in my pack. I don't want any light fingers to walk off with it." Sage moved closer to Betty and gently stroked the old mare's neck. "I guess I didn't hide it well enough."

"*No kidding, Sherlock!*" Tia replied in a fair imitation of Sage's caustic comment. Sage rolled her eyes as Tia went on. "We need to know where everyone else was last night after eleven, and who came through the gates and what time they left. Oh, and we'd better enlist Ty for our team." She pushed open the gate on the box stall.

"Hey, Tia …"

Tia turned back to Sage.

"Thanks."

Tia nodded and left the barn, not sure if she was doing Sage a favour or not.

Chapter 14

As Tia went to find Ty, she noticed two RCMP cruisers parked in front of the admin building. That meant the official questioning had started. She remembered the letter about the case concerning the Denver Way Station for Girls. With experience like that, Ty was sure to have some good advice. She hurried up the admin steps as Ty strode out of the building. "Can I talk to you?"

He must have heard the urgency in her voice. "Over here." They moved to a corner of the wide wrap-around veranda. "Tia, I'm glad you're here." His dark eyes searched hers and she knew he had more bad news.

She glanced at the two police cars; the clock was ticking. "I spoke to Sage and it looks bad, but I'm not sure she did it. Some things don't add up. The problem is that, when the police find out about that pin, I'm sure they won't look any further. I have to find out what happened last night.

Ty, I need your help."

Tia thought she detected a note of impatience when Ty spoke.

"Tia, I was worried the police wouldn't understand about my wine stash, so I went to move it. Imagine my surprise to find someone had already relieved me of both bottles." Tia felt her stomach sink. "I was even more surprised when Emma reported to Dr. Stone that she'd found two empty wine bottles in the barn garbage. Didn't you tell me Sage was there until late last night?"

Tia knew if Sage was innocent of the theft, this wasn't going to help her case, but she couldn't lie. "She admits she took the wine, but swears that's all she helped herself to. It was partly my fault. Sage has self-confidence issues and last night I treated her like she wasn't important. I think she got drunk to show me."

He ran his hand through his hair. "Sage stole my cigarettes, didn't she?"

Tia nodded glumly. "Okay, she's guilty of incredibly poor judgement, but that doesn't automatically mean she took the money. When this comes out, the police will treat it like case over, with Sage as the big loser."

Ty's face looked grim. "Breaking and entering, stealing wine and cigarettes. Do you remember telling me you thought Sage Knowles was a tough case for a first client? It looks like you were right." He hesitated. "Tia, you have a better feel for what Sage is capable of. Do you think she did it?"

Tia wanted to say "No, of course Sage didn't do it," and state without a doubt that her client was innocent. But she couldn't. "I don't know. I want to believe her."

Ty paused. "If I'm asked, I have to tell the police what I know. I'll check with the other trail riders to see if their clients were accounted for last night. Maybe one of their little angels was AWOL." He touched her arm. "Don't look so worried. If someone else took the money, we'll find out who it was. But Tia," he searched for the right words. "If it turns out to be Sage — and it very well could — you can't beat yourself up. This is a girl who is skilled at surviving on the streets by any method, including lying so smoothly her own mother wouldn't know."

As Tia watched Ty walk away, something he said struck her. *Emma had found the empty wine bottles.* Tia knew she'd been careful when she'd hidden the empties. What was Emma doing rooting around in the tack-room garbage?

* * *

Finding Emma wasn't easy. For a girl on crutches, she was darn hard to track down. Tia rounded a thicket of willows and stopped. Emma was coming toward her, but not as Tia expected. Not only didn't Emma have crutches; she wasn't even limping!

"Wow, Emma, your ankle must be feeling a whole lot better." Tia eyed the girl skeptically.

"Just last night, you needed Ty to get your food and help you move around, but this morning you've made a miraculous recovery."

Emma drew herself up, her body language making the challenge plain. "So what? I'm a fast healer."

"I heard you found two empty wine bottles in the barn. How did you happen to come across them?" The question caught Emma off guard.

"I ... uh, I dropped one of my special earrings in the garbage and was looking for it." She fingered her gaudy chandelier earrings.

The teen had taken a heartbeat too long to answer and Tia knew she was lying. "What time did you go to your cabin last night?"

"I don't know. It was right after Sage came by looking really ticked off."

That would have put it after 11.00, because Sage had been at their cabin a couple of minutes before. The angry teen must have been on her way to get the wine. "And were Sara and Meagan there?" Tia pressed.

"Duh, yeah." Emma looked at her like she was an idiot.

Tia glanced down at Emma's ankle. "All right. I'm glad you're okay. Do you know where Sara and Meagan are now?"

"Yeah. Meagan wimped out of breakfast because of a headache so she and Sara are still back at our cabin."

"Thanks." Tia turned away. She would check

with Sara what time Meagan had turned in and when Ty had brought Emma back. Not that she didn't trust Emma … but, well, she didn't trust Emma!

"I was in the barn with Sage a couple of minutes ago." Emma's voice stopped Tia in her tracks and she spun around to see the large girl smirking.

"Is that so?" Tia's tone was deliberately calm. The note of triumph in the teen's voice was unmistakable and Tia knew the trip to the barn hadn't been to take Sage cupcakes.

"I told her Ty was going to rat to the cops that she'd broken into the admin building last night and stole the booze. I also mentioned to little Sage that he would have to say who owned the dragon pin." She went on smugly. "How do I know all this, you ask? I was looking for Ty this morning and happened to be around the corner of the veranda when you two had your tête-à-tête." Her eyes glittered with malice. "They're definitely going to want to know where Sage was last night. You *so* know where she was, right?"

Tia couldn't believe how these girls thought nothing of throwing each other to the wolves. It was like a game to see who could survive the longest before they were torn apart by the hungry pack.

"Where Sage and I were is no concern of yours Emma. What you should be asking yourself is what you'll tell the police when they ask where you were."

Emma's tone was bitter. "Your precious Sage is

playing you. Do you think last night was the only time she was sneaking around? I've seen her creep out of your cabin in the middle of the night plenty of times."

Tia felt her stomach tighten. She thought of the dream she'd had of the cabin door opening and closing. No wonder it had seemed so real! What had Sage been doing?

Tia didn't respond to Emma's taunt. Instead, she turned and continued down the path. She was having second, or maybe it was third, thoughts about believing Sage. Tia felt like the whole thing had become something more, something bigger. Truth and lies, trust and deceit, friend and enemy had all become mixed up together.

Knocking on Sara's cottage door, Tia waited in the warm sunshine. She looked around at the peaceful setting. The cool river and the old barn, the horses quietly milling around in the corral — it was hard to believe anyone from this piece of paradise had stolen the money.

An Alberta wild rose bush beside the door was a mass of deep pink blooms and the scent was wonderful. Tia's eye was caught by something buried in the earth under the bush. Scraping at the soil with the toe of her boot, she uncovered several cigarette butts with bright orange lipstick stains.

Apparently Emma had not only told Sage where the cigarettes were stashed, but had scooped some herself. She stopped. Unless Emma had taken more … What if she'd broken in last night for cigarettes and decided to help herself to the cash? Her fingerprints would weaken the case against Sage. And if Emma had some, there was no way Meagan wasn't in on the contraband too! Maybe she left for a quick smoke last night sometime after 11:00?

Tia covered the butts with her boot as Sara answered the door. They exchanged quick pleasantries, and then Tia cut to the chase. "Hey, Sara, can I ask you what time Meagan went back to your cabin last night?"

Sara thought for a moment. "Around ten after eleven. Meagan was coming down with something and felt crummy, so we decided to call it quits after Ty finished with the campfire singalong."

"And Meagan stayed in all night?" Tia asked.

Sara looked a little sheepish. "I think so. To be honest, I zipped out to meet Sean Hastings, but he stood me up. I was only gone about ten minutes."

"Maybe a little longer ..." Tia grinned conspiratorially, hoping Sara would tell her more.

Her face was flushed and she wouldn't meet Tia's eye. "Yeah, maybe."

Tia made a quick calculation and decided ten minutes wasn't long enough for Meagan to make a trip to the admin building, but thirty or maybe forty certainly put it in the realm of possibility. "So you left Meagan alone in bed for that half-hour or so and she was still there when you got back?"

Sara looked indignant. "No, of course not! I wouldn't have left a sick girl alone for a minute. Emma was with her."

Now it was Tia's turn to be surprised. "Emma was here?"

"Yes, we all came back together." Sara gave her a knowing look. "Speaking of Emma, I think the invalid thing had a lot to do with Ty being her hero. When he stopped fawning over her, the leg miraculously healed."

"Funny how that works." Tia smiled wryly. It was smart of Ty to bring Emma back when he had witnesses. No sense putting himself in harm's way by being alone with an amorous teenager, and there had been no doubt what had been on Emma's mind last night!

"Sara, you missed breakfast to stay with your patient. Why don't I wait with Meagan while you get something to eat?" Tia offered with a friendly smile.

Glancing back at Meagan still asleep in her bunk, Sara seemed about to refuse, then nodded. "You know I could really go for a coffee and some scrambled eggs. I also want to get some ibuprofen and orange juice for Meagan." She opened the screen door wide and Tia stepped in as she stepped out. "I'll be back in no time. Thanks, Tia."

Once Sara left, Tia picked up a large book from the table and moved toward the sleeping girl. Standing right beside Meagan's bed, she dropped the book.

Chapter 15

"What the …!" Meagan shot bolt upright.

"Oh, clumsy me. I'm sorry Meagan! It slipped right out of my hand." Tia looked at Meagan's face. She didn't look sick, just tired, like any teenager who wanted to sleep till noon without anyone bugging her.

Tia put a stop to that idea right away. "Last night was a lot of fun. Did you enjoy yourself?"

Meagan looked at her as though she were speaking Outer Mongolian. "Last night? Yeah, sure, a barrel of laughs." She sat up and yawned. "Where's Sara?"

"She went to get some coffee and drugs for you. She thinks you're coming down with something." Tia sat in a chair by the table. "Emma's leg is much better this morning. In fact, she can walk without crutches."

Meagan snorted. "Big surprise. She could have gone two-stepping last night if Tyler Simmons had asked her."

Obviously Meagan knew Emma had been milking the bad leg thing. "She sure had Ty fooled. Hey, it was too bad you had to come back to the cabin so early, but I bet you were dying for a smoke. It's a dumb rule." Tia leafed through a fashion magazine that was open on the table. Darting a glance at Meagan, she saw that she had the teen's attention. "You know, about not being able to have a cigarette when you absolutely need one."

"That's what I said to Sara! But there was no way she'd let us have a quick puff. She goes on about the evils of wicked tobacco like Mother Theresa." Meagan rolled her eyes.

"Yeah, Sara can be a bit of a hard case. I bet you and Emma have to sneak cigarettes when she's not around, like last night when she left the cabin?" Tia waited. Meagan looked doubtful as though she wasn't sure she could trust Tia. "Oh, by the way, I saw a couple of butts in the dirt outside and covered them up before Sara noticed."

Meagan's face became grim. "I told Emma she was stupid to smoke so close to the cabin. She's going to get us busted."

"Yeah!" Tia concurred. "You're much smarter to smoke away from the place, where there's no chance of evidence being found. You're sure the butts are really out when you ditch them? We don't need a forest fire on this side of the mountain too."

"No worries. I smoke down by the river out of sight of all the cabins." Meagan gave a short bark of a laugh. "Last night after Sara left, I hot-footed it to the creek to have one of the cigarettes Sage had slipped me ..." She smiled at Tia's surprise and her eyes narrowed like a cat playing with a mouse. "Oh, it wasn't only Emma that Sage supplied smokes to."

Tia felt her faith in Sage slip another notch.

"Anyway, you'll never guess." Meagan went on. "I'm busy lighting up and who comes along but our own Nurse Calloway from the infirmary and Doctor Stone, and they weren't down there because they liked the view. Can you believe it? The old geezers were making out, or at least what passes for making out with the over-sixty crowd. I nearly got caught and had to stand in the bushes for twenty minutes until they left. I barely made it back before Sara came in." They both knew Tia couldn't say anything about this escapade without incriminating Sage.

Meagan stretched and rubbed her hair. "I need a shower. I smell like I've been in the bush for a year after that smoky campfire last night. You don't have to wait. I'll tell Sara I felt fine and told you to take a hike." She climbed down out of her bunk and padded to the bathroom.

Tia closed the cabin door behind her. She'd debated whether to tell Meagan about the theft, then decided not to bother. She'd know soon enough, or perhaps she already knew from first-hand experience. It struck Tia that Meagan might be lying; She hadn't gone for a smoke, but had gone to the admin building instead, then saw Dr. Stone and Nurse Calloway on her way back. Seeing the administrators' tryst didn't prove Meagan had stayed in the bushes for the entire time.

Meagan could have taken the money. Tia put her on the list of suspects, as was Emma, who would have been alone. And now that the ailing girl's miraculous cure could be pushed back to last night, Emma would have been capable of stealing the money while the other two were away.

Another important detail struck her. Not only did both of them have the opportunity, but after the campfire conversation they both knew about Sage's pin and could have planted it to frame her. Neither Emma nor Meagan would have any qualms about sticking the blame on Sage.

Tia had to be honest with herself. Until Sage could explain Emma's revelation about her leaving the cabin at night, her client was also still firmly on that list of suspects. As she walked to the barn, Tia felt caught in a video loop with her repeatedly going back to Sage to explain another hole in her story.

"Sage!" she called as she entered the dimly lit barn with its familiar smells. "We need to talk."

No answer. The place felt deserted.

A bad feeling came over Tia. As she looked at the line of horses contentedly munching on their morning oats, something didn't seem right. Then it hit her like a Mack truck.

Bouncing Betty's stall was empty!

Chapter 16

Tia raced back to their cabin, hoping that Sage would be there, or had simply taken Betty for a short ride. Their cabin door was open, which was odd, as Sage always carefully locked up. Tia walked in and groaned. No Sage. And worse, it quickly became obvious that the meagre possessions her client had brought were also gone. This was disastrous for Sage's case. Innocent people didn't run.

With no time to waste, Tia sprinted for Ty's cabin, praying he'd be there. As she ran, she noticed the smoke in the air was thicker than it had been earlier. She banged on his door and waited. "Come on, come on …"

Finally, Ty opened the door. He must have seen from her face that there was trouble. "What's happened? Did they arrest Sage?"

Tia shook her head. "Worse. Sage is gone."

"What do you mean *gone?*" He looked past her

shoulder as though to check for himself.

"She was afraid she'd be nailed for the theft, so she took Betty and is making a run for it. We need to find her before something awful happens." Tia tried to sound calm, but the catch in her voice gave her away.

"Damn! This is bad, Tia. I talked to John Stone and he told me the fire has shifted and is heading this way. The forest service called and we have to evacuate. All the trail riders are being notified and the authorities are sending buses for us. The trailers for the livestock will be here later." His eyes searched her face. "They may not let us go after her. That would put three lives in jeopardy instead of only one. Sage may be on her own."

Tia thought of the young street teen who acted so tough on the outside but was actually scared inside. Sage, who desperately wanted someone to have faith in her, to believe in her. Then she thought of the Sage who could lie with the face of an angel. "I'm not giving up on her, guilty or innocent. We might be able to save her from the theft charges, but she doesn't stand a chance against that fire. Ty, I've been doing some investigating and have new suspects the police will want to take a hard look at."

"What suspects are you talking about?" Ty asked curiously.

"I'll tell you later. Right now, we have to go after Sage." She felt the jagged edge of panic. This was her fault. She should have been with Sage last night and given her the airtight alibi she desperately needed, or maybe stopped her from committing a terrible mistake.

Ty took her hand. "I've got a plan. I'll go after her while you explain to Dr. Stone what's happened. That way if he says no, it will be too late to rein me in and ..." He gave her a warm smile. "I won't have to worry about you chasing after some wild kid and getting yourself hurt."

Tia knew that Sage was her responsibility, and now was not the time to be over-protective. "Are you kidding? I'm going after her. I let Sage down once; there's no way I'll do it again. Dr. Stone is reasonable. He has to let us both go." Her tone said there was no room for argument. She left to speak to the chief administrator with Ty right behind her.

* * *

"Absolutely not! With the fire headed this way, there's one life in jeopardy now and I can't possibly risk two more." Dr. Stone shook his head adamantly. "I'll alert the forest service to look for her, but we must evacuate."

"But, Dr. Stone, Sage couldn't have gone far. She took Betty because she loves that old mare and knew the horse would listen to her, but they'll be moving slowly." Convincing Dr. Stone wasn't easy. Tia tried again. "If she's taken the main road back to the city, she'll only be a few kilometres away." Tia didn't think Sage was dumb enough to take the well-used route. The streetwise teen knew that would be the first place the authorities would look. However, if Dr. Stone thought it would only be a matter of minutes before they caught her, he might let them go.

"Why not let me track down this runaway, John?" Ty interrupted. "Satan and I could have her back in no time without endangering any more staff than necessary."

Dr. Stone rubbed his eyes wearily. "I've been through a fire before. The destructive power is unbelievable. You have no idea how fast a full-blown forest fire can move. When I think of that young girl out there alone ..." He looked at Ty and he seemed to age before Tia's eyes. "Do you think you could get her, Ty?"

Tia met Ty's gaze and furiously sent him silent signals that he studiously ignored. He was trying to protect her, but he was out of line here. She spoke up. "Excuse me, Dr. Stone, but I want to go after Sage. I know how she thinks." Tia raised her chin and straightened her shoulders. "She's my client and I failed her. I want to make things right between us."

The ranch supervisor hesitated, looking at the map, then at his watch. "The police investigation is ongoing, but until the fire danger is under con-trol, my first priority is the safety of this ranch. Once things are secure, they'll want to talk to the staff and clients — *all* the staff and *all* the clients." He looked meaningfully at Tia and Ty as he came to a decision. "The livestock trucks are on their way. They'll be finished loading the animals in three hours and you could leave with the last of them."

Tia had no idea how long it would take to catch up to Sage, but if three hours was the deadline set, that's the one she'd agree to. "No problem, Dr. Stone."

He pursed his lips. "All right, you can go after her. But I want you both to be perfectly clear on one point — whether you have Sage or not, you must be back here in three hours."

* * *

Tia could feel Blaster's nervousness, just as he sensed her tension. Even a horse his size never forgot it was a prey animal, and the best way to stay alive was to look for the teeth and claws that might be hiding in the bushes. Tia tried to reassure him with gentle words. "It's okay, boy. We'll find her and bring her back, then I'll give you a big bucket of oats and molasses."

As they rode through the gates, the skittish stallion had to be corrected several times. "He's acting like he's barn-sour and wants to stay tucked away safe in his stall." Tia pointed Blaster in the right direction one more time.

"Maybe he knows something we don't!" Ty joked and Tia hoped he wasn't right.

Tia had a hunch where Sage was headed. They started on the road toward Calgary, and then Tia struck out across the brush, making for the trail that would take them to the summer pasturing grounds.

"Hey, where are you going? I thought you told John that Sage was headed to Calgary." Ty nudged Satan forward to catch up to Tia.

"She is, but not on this road. Sage isn't stupid, Ty. She'll know this is the first place we'd look." Tia pushed Blaster harder, covering ground quickly as she told Ty her hunch. "On the cattle drive, Sage was interested in the cable ferry crossing where the rafting company is located. She knows the road on the other side is a shortcut that will halve her time and distance to Calgary."

He looked at her suspiciously. "And how did she find out about the shortcut back to the city?"

Tia's neck felt warm as she admitted the truth. "I guess I told her that bit of local travel information. I didn't think she'd ever get to actually use it."

"If she knows that, I'd say you're probably right. She'll figure out a way to con the ferryman into taking her across once she gets there, or she could steal one of the rafts and take her chances on the river."

"What are we waiting for?" Tia gave the signal to Blaster and the powerful stallion sprinted forward.

* * *

After an hour's ride, they came to a wide trench cut by spring runoff. A fast flowing mountain creek swept along the bottom of the steep-sided gully, splashing white foam on the jagged rocks that lined the wash. The cut extended as far as Tia could see in either direction, making going around out of the question.

"This is a tough one. We'll have to go back and try to find another way." Ty turned Satan.

Tia knew that would take hours. "Wait." She inspected the edge of the drop-off, but the sides were too treacherous to chance the horses picking their way down. She had an idea, but knew Ty wouldn't like it. "There is one way. We can fly over."

Ty looked at her and shook his head. "No way! It's too dangerous."

"Blaster can do it, and you and Satan must have come up against tougher stuff than this. I'm telling you, we can do it." She turned Blaster back along the path to give him room to get up speed. Horse and rider faced the chasm.

Tia shortened her reins as she directed her big stallion toward the edge of the drop off. "You heard what I told the man. We can do this," she whispered. Closing her legs around the horse, she urged him forward. Blaster trusted her and responded to the signal. Without hesitating, he ran toward the edge of the ravine. Tia felt him gather his strong muscles for the jump. With a mighty leap, the huge animal spanned the distance in a graceful movement that was smooth and effortless.

"I think you're crazy!" Ty called as he and Satan followed. Horse and rider cleared the wide chasm, but only barely. A foot shorter and it would have been disaster. Ty looked back and whistled. "Let's not make a habit out of that!" He looked around and then pointed to the steep ridge ahead. The hill was shrouded in thick blue smoke. "If we ride over that whaleback, we should come out upstream of the ferry crossing."

Neck reining her horse, Tia turned him and started up the slope that led to the ridge. "There's only one small problem." Leaning forward in the saddle, she distributed her weight to make it easier for Blaster to climb the steep hill. "The fire's coming straight down that river valley."

Chapter 17

The climb up to the ridge was arduous. Several times Tia and Ty had to dismount and lead their horses through the tangled deadfall, or coax them across streams now choked with blackened skeletons of what were once towering pines.

When they reached the top, they stopped to survey the valley below. In places the river was partially hidden by a thick blanket of smoke, and the air was hot, as though someone had opened an oven door. As their gaze travelled further up the valley, the reason became clear.

A brilliant wall of fire moved toward them at a frightening speed. As they watched, flame leaped up the sides of mountains, clawing its way around boulders as though it was a starving army in search of food.

"I'd say we better not waste any time finding Sage." Tia stared at the undulating curtain of flame as though mesmerized.

"If the wind shifts, we'll never be able to out-run it." Ty looked at her and she knew what he would say next. "Tia, if we can't find her on the first try, we're not going to have the luxury of a second. We'll have to get out fast."

Tia turned away, knowing what that meant for Sage.

They started down, sinking deeper and deeper into the thick acrid air. The horses laboured in the choking smoke until Tia stopped at a small stream seeping out of a crack in a rock face and dismounted.

"This smoke is going to kill the horses." Her eyes stung as she removed her hoodie, then secured the thin jacket around Blaster's eyes. After tearing the bottom off her T-shirt, she soaked the wide strip of cloth in the water before tying it around the horse's nose. "This should help with the smoke." She removed the hoodie and rubbed Blaster's cheek. "You look styling, boy." Her tone was low and comforting and the horse soon accepted his new headgear.

Assured her horse was okay with the makeshift mask, Tia shredded another piece of material and did the same for herself.

Ty followed Tia's lead. As he finished tying a piece of his shirt around Satan's nose, he looked at the ash and smoke swirling in the air. "Let's hope we can find Sage in all this mess."

"We will. We have to." Tia was grim as she remounted and plunged into the curtain of smoke.

Following the river, Tia knew the ferry crossing

was not far away. She wondered if this was a needless trip for her and Ty. Maybe the ferryman saw the fire coming and had left with Sage. "There's the crossing up ahead!" she called hoarsely as she scanned the riverbank. The ferryboat was moored on the far side and there were no rafts anywhere. The place looked deserted.

Then Tia spotted Sage standing near the river's edge with her horse. "She's beside the ferry!"

She urged Blaster forward, waving until she caught Sage's attention. "Where's the ferryman?" she called across the wide stream. "We need to get you and Betty over to this side *now*. The fire's headed this way!"

Sage looked exhausted and scared. "The guy who runs this thing is gone and I don't know how to get it back over." She pointed at the barge.

Ty looked at the silt-brown water carrying smouldering trees and tangles of burnt branches. "She'll have to swim her horse over here."

Tia looked at Sage and her old mare, then back to Ty. "Sage isn't an experienced enough rider and Betty's too old. Either Sage or Betty, or maybe both, will drown. We have to go to them and try to get the ferry running."

Ty looked at the swollen river, choked with debris. "This is not going to be easy."

"We stand a better chance than Sage. She can barely sit a horse, let alone handle a dangerous crossing like this." Tia nudged Blaster toward the edge of the wide stream. "Here's where you get to show off, boy." She knew her horse could handle the water. He'd never shied from a good dunking in his life. Blaster plunged into the stream as though it was a reward for good behaviour. Satan and Ty were right behind them.

The crossing was brutally hard. Several times Tia had to hold Blaster back or turn him aside while a burning branch floated by on the churning current. Her grip was tight on the saddle horn as the powerful horse pushed forward.

Finally, Blaster heaved himself out of the water carrying Tia, soaked and soggy, with him. He was winded from the exertion and Tia didn't feel much better. The muscles in her shoulders ached from gripping the saddle horn.

Ty and Satan thrashed out of the water behind her, struggling up the bank. Catching his breath, Ty dismounted. "Are all dates with you like this?"

"Once this is over, you'll have to find out," Tia smiled.

"I'll hold you to that. But right now, I have to see to that ferry's engine."

He handed Tia his reins and she watched as he walked away. She still found him incredibly appealing, even wet and dripping in the middle of a forest fire.

Sage ran toward Tia, the mare reluctantly in tow. "That was amazing! But if you think old Betty and I can do that, you're on drugs! I can't freakin' swim and she doesn't want to!"

Tia thought Sage's bravado would have been

more believable if it weren't for the tear streaks down her sooty cheeks. "Don't worry, we'll take the ferry back." She scanned the deserted landing. "Why didn't you go with the ferryman? You must have known the fire was coming this way."

Sage laid a protective hand on Betty's neck. "He had a car and the jerk said to leave Betty and go with him. There was no way I could desert my best friend." She buried her face in the mare's neck and Betty responded by nuzzling the girl's hair. "I sort of flipped out, then told him to take a hike. He said he'd notify the authorities I was here, but he wasn't waiting around to be barbecued. After he left, the fire cut off the road and we were trapped."

Tia could see the bonding process between horse and rider had worked, perhaps too well. Sage had been willing to risk her life rather than leave Betty behind. It was a decision she knew the runaway wouldn't have made a few weeks ago.

"Come on, let's see if Ty can crank up our ride home." They started toward the shed, where sounds of clanking and cursing could be heard.

Ty emerged as they walked up. "This whole thing keeps getting better and better. The ferryman locked everything down before he left, and I can't get the generator to work." He tossed a set of large pliers into the dirt. "We have no choice but to swim back."

Sage blanched. "I, I … can't," she stuttered. "I wasn't kidding when I said I don't swim." Her voice was edged with panic.

It was then they heard it. It sounded like a

diesel locomotive roaring toward them. Tia looked up to see an astonishing sight. The fire leaped from treetop to treetop as it flashed overhead with amazing speed. Pine needles crackled, then exploded into flame. Fear clutched at Tia's throat as a scorching wind roared over her. "Oh, my God!" she whispered.

As they watched, the flames jumped the river and ignited the trees on the other side. Building roofs smouldered as sparks fell like molten lava. Before they could react, the tinder-dry pines erupted into towering torches and the blistering heat sucked the air out of their lungs. The fire had surrounded them.

The horses pulled frantically on the reins as their flight instinct took over.

Blaster, pushed beyond his limits, reared and kicked out with razor-sharp front hooves. In all the years Tia had owned the big stallion, he'd never reared before. "They're losing their minds!" she shouted. "We've got to get them out of here."

But where would they go? Flames blocked every avenue of escape. Damn that stupid ferry! Tia thought as she stared at the useless flat-bottomed boat.

Then it hit her. It was a boat! A big floating platform really, but one designed to be in the water with a heavy cargo on board. "Ty, can you get rid of the cable so the ferry will float freely?"

He frowned. "Why on earth do you want me to do that?"

"Because that's how we're getting out of here."

Then he understood. "Are you nuts? There's no way you'll get those panicked horses onto that thing. We should turn them loose and let them run."

Tia looked at Sage, who was now wide-eyed with terror. The scared teen shook her head adamantly and clutched Betty's mane.

"We're all going on the ferry, including the horses." Tia quickly sketched out her plan. "We'll blindfold the horses, then load them onto the ferry. Using a couple of those trees," she pointed to a pile of neatly stacked logs, "we'll barge pole down the river like Tom Sawyer on the mighty Mississippi. We can wet everything down and make a run through the gauntlet of fire. It's crazy, but it might work."

Ty still didn't look convinced.

"If you have a better plan, I'm willing to listen, but you better make it fast!" Tia glanced at the far building that was now burning.

Cursing, Ty went back to the engine shack and came out with a large wrench. "The pulley assembly is bolted to the floor. If I can break it loose, I can push it overboard, and that will free the boat." He ran to the barge and began working on the bolts that secured the steel cable housing.

Tia and Sage found suitably stout logs to act as steering and poling tools, then Tia started toward the horses. "Come on, let's get these guys loaded."

The horses had other ideas. They were spooked by the smells and sounds all around them. Even blindfolded, weren't about to walk onto a floating paddock. Tia and Sage prodded and pushed until finally Betty and Satan were aboard. Blaster, however, steadfastly refused to have anything to do with Tia's coaxing.

"You are such a greenhorn," Sage said to Tia. She took something out of one of the pockets of her old army jacket and held it out to Blaster, who sniffed and curled his lips as he reached for her hand. She gave him a small piece, then pulled back as the big stallion moved in for more. "Not so fast, big fella. Business first. Come on." Holding her hand out in front of his nose, she backed up the ramp onto the boat as Blaster docilely followed. Once she had him securely tied, she offered him the rest of the magic item in her palm. Blaster greedily ate the mysterious treat.

"What was that?" Tia asked, amazed.

Sage grinned. "Black licorice. He loves it. I discovered his sweet tooth when Betty and I were visiting. He stuck his big ol' head over the stall and tried to take it right out of my hand. I shared, and we've been buddies ever since."

Speechless, Tia could only smile. Sage was full of surprises and so was Blaster! The two girls finished tightening the safety lines on the horses just as Ty shoved the large mechanical wheels overboard.

"It's now or never!" With one last look at the burning buildings, Tia picked up her pole and pushed the boat into the racing current.

Chapter 18

"Watch out for that boulder!" Tia yelled as she pushed against the large rock with her pole. They were in the heart of a vicious section of rapids and the ferry wasn't designed to handle rough water.

"I'll try to shove it off the bottom and pivot around the rock!" Ty drove his pole down and the boat skirted the jagged boulder, narrowly missing a collision.

The strong current pulled at the ferry, sucking it downstream as Ty and Tia struggled to maintain the little control they had. The trees overhead roared with flame as Sage, who'd tied the horses to the side rails, busily kept everything dripping wet by scooping up water in an old bucket she'd found.

Water washed over the edge of the flat-bottomed boat, making the greasy surface slippery. Several times Tia nearly fell when her riding boot hit a patch of slimy wet oil left from years of transporting old cars and rusty trucks.

The fire moved rapidly on either side of the river now, and the smoke was so dense it made seeing what lay ahead impossible. Tia remembered telling Sage this was a Class 4 river — a really rough ride.

Up ahead, the river cut between the steep sides of a narrow canyon, making it seem like they were going into the gates of Hell, trees blazing furiously on either side of the dangerous portal. The current picked up as foam-white waves hit the front of the boat sending spray sheeting over them.

"Sage, grab onto something!" Tia yelled and Sage wrapped her arms around one of the side rails.

"This is going to be close!" Ty called. "Tia, have your pole ready to push us off the walls. We need to stay in the middle where it's deepest!"

Tia braced herself as the ferry started down the fast flowing chute. One wave hit so hard, icy shards of spray showered her whole body, taking her breath away. At the entrance to the narrow crevasse, Tia glimpsed sharp spikes of rock sticking out of the churning water like dragon's teeth. "Ty! Those rocks are going to trap us! We've got to get over to the far wall of the canyon!"

Together, they coaxed and cajoled the big raft, straining to divert its course, but the current was too strong. As the grim jaws neared, Ty gave his pole one last mighty pull. The boat groaned, then grudgingly moved away from the dangerous rocks, narrowly missing the deadly stone net.

Tia heard the raft scrape the rocks hidden beneath the water. If they got hung up here, they were in trouble. They were smack in the middle of the narrow gorge with steep walls and rushing water all around. Shoving on the pole with all her might, she felt the raft start to lift off and float free once more. She pushed until her shoulder muscles screamed from the exertion.

With a sudden crack, the pole snapped in two, nearly sending her into the river. She groped for the edge of the guardrail that ran down the two sides of the raft. Her hands were wet and the rail slippery. She yelled as her hand closed around thin air.

In a lightning fast move, Ty reached out and grabbed her, pulling her back from the edge. Tia felt his arms go around her. Her hands were shaking as she took a deep breath. "That was way too close! I could have been killed. Thanks!"

"Anytime," he smiled down at her.

"Hey, you guys! Look! We've made it!" Sage pointed to the exit of the narrow crevasse. Beyond, the river opened out and seemed to calm itself.

As they emerged from the canyon, the air cleared. Tia looked around. The trees here were untouched by the terrible inferno behind them. "We've outrun it!" She hugged Ty. "We can stay on the raft and float right past the ranch. With a little creative poling, we might even park at the dock."

Tia and Sage checked the horses to make sure they'd come through the ordeal safely. Satisfied the animals were okay, they sat on the floor of the barge. The river was doing most of the work now, and all Ty had to do was use his pole to keep the barge in the middle of the current.

"I still don't want to go back." Sage squeezed some water out of her soggy pant legs. "The cops will bust me the second I step off this boat."

"Sometimes, it's best to admit your guilt, Sage." Ty looked down at her. "Tia and I can put in a good word for you. You'll get a reduced sentence." His tone was sympathetic.

Sage shook her head. "You don't get it. *I didn't do it!*"

Ty looked at her sadly. "The evidence doesn't say that."

"I don't care what the friggin' evidence says." Sage looked at Ty defiantly. "I was framed!"

"Okay, okay. Let's keep our heads." Tia motioned for both of them to settle down. "Sage is right. Once we get back to the ranch, the police will want to talk to her. I'm sure they've found out about the pin by now, and probably about her private party too." She'd been mulling everything over in her head, trying to make sense out of it. "Let's work together to try to figure this out. Sage, last night, did you hang out with anyone?" She hoped Sage would say yes, that she'd spent hours having a great time with one of the girls. Instead, Sage tipped her head until her hair fell in front of her face, hiding it from Tia.

"I tried to talk to you, but you told me to take a hike."

Tia felt a sharp arrow of guilt. "I screwed up. I'm sorry, Sage." She cleared her throat, swallowing the lump that had formed there. "Hey, I haven't told you what I discovered. I've uncovered some important information the police will be very interested in — like the fact there were at least two other people who could have been in the admin building at the time of the robbery."

Sage's head came up. "Really?"

Sage looked at her, red-eyed. "Really?"

"Really," Tia said with a smile. "Ty, you'll want to hear this too."

Ty continued to watch the river for snags. "Okay, what have you got?" He shoved on the pole to keep the barge from drifting too far out of the current.

Tia explained what she'd found out about Emma and Meagan. "Emma wasn't laid up on her bad ankle. She could have gone to the admin building, no problem; plus she knew her way around once inside."

Sage was instantly excited. "Right — I know she's been there before to *borrow* some of Ty's cigarettes." She gave Ty a coy smile. The ranch is full of talented kids."

Tia went on, "Then there's Meagan, who was away from the cabin for a long smoke, but no one saw her. Both girls had convenient windows of at least a half-hour unaccounted for."

"We'll never be able to prove which one did it." Sage sounded defeated.

"Sage, it's not our job to find out who really did it. That's for the police. The big thing is that I think these new suspects provide a ton of doubt that it was you. Once we tell all this to the police, they'll keep looking for the real thief."

"But the deck's stacked against me," Sage's voice cracked. "It was my pin they found. I'm the one with a rap sheet as thick as a phone book and no one to alibi me except old Betty. Even then, where I was and what I was doing might not work in my favour." She looked across the water, her face a mask of defeat. "Loser with a capital *L*."

"Don't give up so easily. The pin might help us. Who knew you had it?" Tia asked.

"It's not something I spread around. The other kids at the ranch aren't exactly Snow White." Sage thought a moment. "I guess the only people who knew where the ones at the campfire. Remember Emma and her fashion advice?"

Tia remembered discussing the pin. "Okay. They're the same top two candidates on our hit list. That's good. We also have witnesses who can say you *weren't* wearing it that night."

"Right!" Sage agreed. "But our cabin is kept locked and the other girls couldn't snag a key. Trail riders are the only ones who could get at the spares."

It struck Tia that this was the one point she had not given much thought to. As she mulled it over now, the full importance of it hit her. Sage was right. Only trail riders could get at the spare cabin keys, and that meant there were two more suspects to add to her list.

Tia was stunned by the implications. How well did she really know Sara? Or Ty, for that matter? But she couldn't very well accuse Ty there and then, not when he was calmly poling them to safety.

Tia spoke slowly, trying to hide the direction her thoughts were racing. "Sara told me she left the cabin to meet Sean last night after dropping off the girls. But he stood her up, so she has no one to vouch for her whereabouts."

"I know Sara had cash flow problems," Ty added. "She'd been to see her banker recently."

Sage's head came up at this revelation. "No kidding! Let's look at this like a cop bucking for a promotion. Sara was away from the cabin at exactly the right time, which gives her opportunity. And she needed money, that's motive."

Ty looked thoughtful. "Plus she knew her way around the admin building! Sounds like game, set, and match to me."

Tia noticed how quick Ty was to support the idea that Sara was the thief. Would he have been able to frame Sage just as easily? She felt her own self-confidence slip. "I don't know." She couldn't think straight. "I can't make it work in my head.

Sara is the last person I would have thought could do this."

"That may be what she's counting on," Ty offered logically. "She's so obvious you missed her, but thinking about it … Tia, it makes sense."

Tia found herself shaking her head. "Even nicely laid out like that it still doesn't seem right to me. I'm not liking her for it. I feel like I'm missing something. "I'm not liking her for it. I guess I simply don't want it to be her."

"I think you're getting soft," Sage said dejectedly.

The silence on the barge went on for several minutes until Sage finally sighed. "Okay, Tia. I'm with you. Sara's cool and it would bite if it was her, but if it wasn't, then who else would need cash badly enough to risk jail if they got busted? Maybe a big spender or someone bankrolling a third-world country?"

Tia pondered Sage's question. Who *would* need the money that badly? "Maybe not a big spender so much as a high roller." She turned to Ty but avoided his eyes. "Do you know anyone who gambles a lot?"

Ty shifted against the steering pole he'd been leaning on and looked away. "Gambling?" He rubbed his lips. "No, I haven't a clue." He shook his head, then quickly glanced down at the water rushing past as he adjusted the pole once more.

A bell jangled in Tia's memory. She watched Ty working the pole, looking down and to his left.

"Wait a minute." Sage jumped up, interrupting Tia's thoughts. "Ty, remember the day of the branding. You signed those forms for Dr. Stone and *gave* me your pen. It had a logo on it, *The River Club*. The River Club is where guys with big bucks go to play poker in high stakes games. Everyone on the street is up on that. Why did you have one of their pens?"

Tia saw the runaway's instinct for survival kick in. In Sage's world, no one was above suspicion and you never showed mercy.

Ty laughed. "I don't know where that pen came from. It was in the office and I happened to pick it up. Maybe Sara left it on the desk."

Sage turned away. "Yeah, Sara." She moved closer to Betty and stroked the horse's neck. "We know Emma, Meagan, or Sara could have done the deed. They left the party early. I saw the three of them going back to their cabin when I was heading to the barn."

"Don't you mean four?" Tia interrupted. "Ty was helping Emma."

Sage looked at her confused. "No, I didn't see him. It was just the three of them."

Tia remembered what Sara had said. *We all came back together.* She had assumed Ty had been with them. Tia looked at Ty. "Is this true?"

"Last night …" Ty rubbed his chin. "Oh, yeah, come to think of it, I guess they did help Emma back without me. I remember now. I didn't want my guitar to get damaged, so I took it to my cabin after our sing-along. My mistake." He smiled, embarrassed at his own fallibility.

Tia frowned, trying to recall a detail. She knew it was important, but couldn't make her brain dredge it up. There was one thing she'd meant to ask Sage and, since they were filling in all the blanks, now was a good time.

"Sage, there's something else I have to ask you and I want a straight answer. Have you ever left the cabin at night without telling me?"

The question caught Sage completely off guard, and then her face flushed. "Who told you that?"

"Just answer my question. If you have and it comes out in court that you regularly went out to do who knows what, and I didn't know about it, it will make things worse."

Sage started to deny it, then looked Tia straight in the eye. "Okay, okay, you busted me. I did leave a few times, but all I did is go to the barn to check on Betty. She gets lonely and wants company. I swear." She drew her legs up and hugged her knees to her chest. "That was why I was with her last night. She was really bummed." Sage looked down at her soot-covered hands.

Tia had wanted Sage to bond with her horse. She had. It didn't take a PhD to see that it was Sage who got lonely. After Tia shut her out, she'd turned to the one friend who had time for her, Betty.

It came back to Tia in a rush. She remembered what it had felt like to be not just alone, but lonely.

Years of always being the kid who didn't fit in, the one others acted differently around. Included but not accepted because she didn't look like all the rest. She'd fought the loneliness by throwing herself into her schoolwork. Sage had chosen a different path.

If this had been a case out of one of her textbooks, Tia would have said the counsellor was being snowed and would be a gullible fool to believe a story like this one. But this wasn't a textbook. This was real life, Sage's life. Maybe it was time to toss the textbook and take a leap of faith, trust her instincts. And her instincts told her that neither Sara nor Sage had done this crime.

Everything they had talked about swirled in Tia's mind. Like pieces of a jigsaw, random bits of information that she thought meant nothing started to come together. Something about the guitar ... What was it?

With a jolt, she remembered. Ty had said he was taking the guitar back to the cabin and that was why he hadn't escorted Emma. Tia had seen that guitar still at the deserted campfire when she went looking for Sage! She glanced at Ty as the details started to click.

Ty knew about the pin, had access to the admin building, and could get a spare key to Tia's cabin. And now he had lied about his guitar! After dropping by last night, he knew Sage had not been with Tia and would have no alibi.

It made perfect sense. Her stomach felt sick.

With a cold certainty she knew she had found her thief. One thing was for certain — she couldn't let Sage down again even if it meant sending Ty to jail.

Tia was now certain she was the wrong person to be there. The problem was that Ty was extremely clever and would have no trouble talking his way out of this. What she needed was for him to tip his hand.

When she was a little girl she'd gone hunting with her father, and he'd always told her, "the bigger the bait, the better the trap." To get the hard proof she was after, she'd need the biggest bait ever

She looked at Sage, who'd pulled her precious camera out and was checking it for damage. *Sage and her camera that she took everywhere with her.* A crazy idea came to Tia. She needed evidence no jury could disregard. Solid photographic proof would be perfect. And if photographic proof didn't exist, Ty didn't have to know that! "Hey, Sage, did your camera make it through this okay?"

She turned to Sage. "Hey, did your camera make it through all this okay?"

Sage pulled the small device out of her vest, absently fiddling with the dials. "Seems okay. I guess the wild ride didn't finish it off. Cool." Her voice sounded relieved. "I've got a lot of memories stored on this thing."

Tia looked at the camera. "When you were wandering around the night of the dance, did you shoot any pictures up by the admin building?"

"Yeah, I think so. Why?"

"It's a long shot, but if you were at the building a little after eleven, on your way to *borrow* the booze ..." She raised an eyebrow.

Sage was up to speed in a flash. "Maybe I recorded someone hanging around the building with something else on their mind!"

They spent the next few minutes watching minuscule images on the tiny screen. Tia saw the night of the barbecue through Sage's eyes. She saw people enjoying the evening, laughing, talking, and dancing, but always from a distance. Sage was never part of it, but stood on the outside looking in with her camera. Tia felt a wave of protectiveness for Sage. Once, she had been that girl looking in too.

The image on the screen became familiar. "That's it!" Tia said excitedly. "The admin building. Can you tell what time that was?"

Sage nodded. "Those little numbers in the corner give the date and time. It's kind of like keeping a diary, but without all the stupid writing."

They stared at the images. A group of girls was sitting at a picnic table with lanterns softly illuminating their faces as they sang.

Tia looked up at Ty. "Exactly where was the pin found?"

Ty shook his head. "Ah, I'm not sure. No, Stone never said."

Tia didn't believe this. She took the camera from Sage and stood up. "I want to check something." She adjusted the dials and studied the tiny screen. "There, in the background behind the girls. I can't make out who it is, but someone's definitely there by the building. It could be the thief planting the phoney evidence! We'll turn the camera over the RCMP. I watch *CSI* on TV, and those crime scene investigators can do miracles. They'll be able to sharpen the image so we can see who it is! Girlfriend, this gizmo is going to bust your case wide open."

Sage smiled with relief. "Hey, maybe getting back to the ranch won't be such a bad thing after all!"

Tia thought Ty would do something, make a grab for the camera, but all he did was turn away and shove on the pole to keep the ungainly boat in the middle of the stream. Satan, who was tied up on the side of the barge, began pulling and stamping his feet.

"Tia, can you have a look at Satan's lead?" Ty called. "He's getting a little antsy and we don't need him breaking free."

Disappointed at the lack of response from Ty, Tia went to check the big gelding's rope.

At that moment, the ferry smashed into a huge boulder that was submerged just below the surface of the river. Tia lurched forward. Over her shoulder, she caught a glimpse of Ty as he fell heavily against Satan. The horse's huge body shifted, slamming into Tia. Skidding on the greasy deck, she desperately tried to steady herself. Ty grabbed for her as she teetered on the edge of the slimy platform, but he was too late.

Tia lost her footing and fell backward into the river.

Chapter 19

"Ty, help me!" Tia screamed as she tried to pull herself back onto the boat.

Ty tossed his pole on the deck and dropped to his stomach. He grabbed for her arm. "Drop the camera and give me your hand!"

"No! We need the evidence!" Tia gasped. She was reaching out to grab hold of the edge when, with a jerk, Ty yanked the camera away and tossed it onto the deck behind him. He grabbed her with both hands and dragged her onto the boat.

Wiping the water from his face, Ty stood up. As he did, Tia heard a crunching sound. She looked down and saw the camera crushed under his boot.

"No!" With a cry of pain, Sage rushed over and knelt beside what was her life's diary, now a pile of smashed plastic and glass "My camera! You broke my camera!" She rocked back and forth.

"I didn't see it. I'm sorry, Sage." Ty turned to Tia. "I know without it, Sage's case will be impossible to prove, but we'll try to find another way to help her."

Tia's eyes met his. Slowly, she climbed to her feet and moved away from Ty. "Sage, come over here." There was authority in Tia's voice. Casually, she bent down and picked up the broken piece of oar that lay on the deck. Sage looked at her like she was cracked, but did as she was told. "Sage, we forgot to list one other person as a suspect." She never took her eyes off Ty. "Tyler Simmons could easily have stolen the money. The pen, the key, the pin — it all fits, not to mention he had lots of opportunity last night. "

Ty looked shocked. "Are you out of your mind? I didn't steal that money and your wanting Sage to be innocent doesn't mean she is. The evidence says she did it."

Tia shook her head sadly. "Satan bumping into me wasn't an accident, was it Ty?" She tightened her grip on the oar. "I needed some tempting bait and thought video proof would work nicely. You were worried about what that camera would show. You knew who'd be in the background planting that pin, so you had to destroy it. I ran a simple psych experiment on you, Ty. I provided the stimulus and you responded in a predictable manner. The funny thing is, there was nothing on that camera. Just a lonely girl's record of a night she wasn't part of."

Tia pinned him with her eyes. "Bells have been going off in my brain. You were sending me signals that I was too slow to pick up on. The way you rubbed your mouth and hesitated when you answered, and then you avoided eye contact and looked down — textbook body language for a liar!"

"You're a first-year psych student. Is it possible you mixed up those body language signals?" His tone was flint edged. "You mixed up the ones that said I was interested in you."

Tia felt her face flush. She'd been pretty sure he really liked her. Maybe her decision to deny her attraction to Ty had made her blind to what was really going on too.

Angrily, Sage shoved past Tia. "You freakin' creep! I'm going to put your lights out!" Tia grabbed her before she got too close to Ty, then pushed the smaller girl behind her. Sage wasn't through yelling. "You set me up, you jerk! I'd have gone to jail for a million years for a theft you did!"

Ty ignored Sage, dismissing her as though she didn't exist. "You know me, Tia. I'm not the bad guy here."

Tia could have laughed. That was the biggest lie of all. "You came by my cabin and I was alone, which meant Sage was unaccounted for. I think you went to the barn and saw she was drunk. That made it easy for you. She was the perfect patsy to take the blame and I was so stupid … If I'd done my job, it would have made it a lot harder for you to frame her."

"Tia, you feel guilty for failing Sage. Your desire to make it up to her has clouded your judgement. I didn't steal that money." Ty's voice was persuasive as he turned slightly and took another step toward her.

She couldn't believe it! He was using the same techniques she did when working with a wary horse! Tia pointed the broken oar at his chest. "It won't work on me, Ty. You wanted to go after Sage alone today, you even tried to cut me out in front of Dr. Stone. Were you planning on a little accident, or were you going to leave her back there to burn?'

"All I was trying to do was help her. I care about these kids, Tia." His voice was sincere, but she saw the muscles in his shoulders tense. He took another step toward her.

She made a threatening poke with the jagged piece of wood and Ty stopped. He stared at her, and Tia saw something new and frightening in his eyes — an icy coldness that made her shiver.

His mouth twisted, all pretence of innocence gone. "You're a very good student, Tia. You figured it out perfectly. I have a few debts that needed to be paid, and my poker buddies don't like waiting for what's owed to them. I had to come up with a lot of cash and the money was sitting there doing nothing. I decided the old barn would do for one more year." His voice lost its soothing tone and became a low growl. "But you were too clever for your own good, and now …" He looked down at the rushing water. With a lightning fast move, Ty lunged for the oar in Tia's hands.

"I don't think so!" Tia gritted her teeth and brought the sturdy piece of log up hard, catching him under the chin. Blood gushed from a ragged cut as the wood sliced open his skin. Ty grunted and went down.

Tia had been standing on a greasy section of the deck. When she connected with Ty, the impact caused her to lose her balance. Her feet went out from under her and she fell, dropping the piece of oar. She looked over at Ty as he lurched toward her. The hateful expression on his bloody face left no doubt what would happen next. Tia reached for the oar, but Ty was faster. He wrenched it from her grasp.

"Hold it right there, you jerk!" Sage darted forward to stand protectively over Tia. She brandished a half-metre piece of rusted pipe from a broken section of the railing. "I've met some creeps on the street, but you win hands down! I would have gone to jail for years while you kept on screwing with kids' lives." Her grip tightened on the pipe. "You should know that there were a lot of assaults not listed on my juvee sheet. All part of living on the street. Like they say, it's a jungle out there."

Time stood still for a heartbeat as the two faced each other. To Tia, they looked like David and Goliath — Sage, small, slim, and delicate against Ty, big, brawny, and bloody.

Tia knew she had only seconds. "Sage, listen to me. He's not worth it. We have him. Together, our testimony will put him away." She got slowly to her feet. "It's two against scum!" Her lame joke seemed to break through to Sage, who grimaced and glanced over at her.

"Of all the counsellors in the world, I get stuck with one who wants to be a stand-up comic." She turned back to Ty.

At that moment, a flash of colour downstream caught Tia's eye. "Look! It's the ranch and there's a crowd waiting for us! You're too late, Ty. There's too many witnesses now."

Sage and Ty both followed Tia's gaze. There, waiting on the dock, was Dr. Stone, and he wasn't alone. There were also several RCMP officers.

"Right on! For once the cops actually show up when I want them to!" Sage handed Tia the pipe and grinned. "You watch him, I'll handle this from here." With newly found confidence, she picked up Ty's pole and began pushing the unwieldy boat toward the shore.

Chapter 20

"I know it's hard to believe, but Ty has been doing this same trick for years. There are at least six cases being reopened at institutions like Ravenhill and the Denver Way Station for Girls where he's worked," Tia told Sage as she handed her a soft brush. She watched as the teen lovingly stroked Betty's coat. "Despite what they teach us, maybe it's true, a leopard never changes its spots."

Several days had passed since the terrible rafting trip and life was returning to normal. The fire hadn't made it to the valley where the ranch was nestled, and the evacuation had been cancelled.

"I think the RCMP investigation answered most of the questions, and I know the rest." Sage replied as she continued to brush Betty, who was now so relaxed she was practically asleep on her four feet. "Since I'd ticked off both Emma and Meagan, and neither had alibis for the time of the theft, they were happy I was going to be hung out to dry." She smoothed a tangle on Betty's mane. "I still think you should have told the cops about them breaking into the admin centre for smokes. It would have served them right."

Tia again thought of how easily loyalties could shift. "Hey, I have no proof they ever broke in. The only person I know of for sure is you, and you admitted to sharing the cigarettes with both Emma and Meagan. You should be ashamed, leading the poor things *ashtray* like that." She paused as Sage groaned at her bad joke. "Besides, they got a letter of reprimand in their file for smoking. Both those ladies are masters at working the system. They joined a Stop Smoking program, so only one extra month was tacked onto their stay here. When Dr. Stone heard how easy it was to break into the admin building, he had a new security system installed. I think he knows you weren't the only night visitor."

Sage's forehead creased. "Emma was the worst. She saw me going to the barn with the wine and knew I stayed there drinking. She was mad at you for flirting with Ty and thought if I was tossed as a thief, you'd be sent packing too. I heard she's going to a foster home, and both her new parents are Calgary police detectives." She wiggled her eyebrows at Tia. "Ironic, huh?"

Tia remembered standing at the cabin door where Emma had been smoking that night. Emma had a clear view to the barn and would have seen Sage heading there with her portable party. That was how she knew to check the trash for empties.

Sage continued. "Sara made up with her crush, who told the cops her meeting was legit. Everyone screwed up, but it wouldn't have mattered except for the theft."

Again, Tia marvelled at how fast news travelled. Sara had told her she was back with Sean only this morning. "Hey, remember, Ty's the real villain. It tears me up when I think of all the young lives he's ruined." Tia felt a tightness in her throat. "I thought he liked me more than he did. I must have seemed as gullible as Emma to him." She felt foolish admitting this to Sage, but somehow during the last few days they'd become close friends, girlfriends.

"Don't sweat it. We all make mistakes, some bigger than others." Sage's eyes were full of regret.

Sage had told the RCMP her story and Tia had interceded with Dr. Stone on her client's behalf. Instead of going to the Young Offenders Centre, Sage would be spending a lot longer at the ranch, but she conceded that it was only fair. She'd messed up. Tia was had been proud of her for accepting the consequences for everything she'd done. She stroked Betty's neck. "Have you talked to your parents about this?"

When Sage raised her big periwinkle eyes, Tia saw something different in them. They were no longer the eyes of a scared runaway teen who couldn't handle her world. This girl radiated self-confidence.

"You know what? I did. In fact, I phoned and

invited them here to have a family conference. We have a lot to discuss." She kissed Betty on the nose. "Like if I can have a pony when I go home. Because that's what I want to do, go home that is, after my *vacation* here is over." She smiled wryly. "I was seriously going to see if I could buy Betty, but then I thought the old girl might not like leaving her four-legged buds or having to get used to a new cramped home, especially after they build the primo barn. I hope they give her the Queen's Suite, she deserves it. Hey, maybe you could find out if Betty ever had any kids?"

"Only if you stop feeding the horses black licorice. It's bad for their teeth."

Tia watched Sage with Betty, and realized it was the horse that had made all the difference. After everything they'd been through, she was now even more confident she'd made the right choice to specialize in Equine Facilitated Counselling. The strength of the trust that had formed between Sage and her horse had amazed Tia. She'd been willing to sacrifice herself for the animal and then had expanded that trust to Tia when she'd defended her. Sage was proof EFC worked, and Tia felt proud that she and Betty had been able to help Sage come back from the edge of disaster.

"Hey, can I ask you something?" Tia asked Sage.

"Sure, what's up?" Sage continued to work on Betty's coat.

"On the ferry, you came to my rescue and

threatened Ty with the pipe. Would you have done it? You know, hit him?" Tia waited to hear what her client would say. Sage was a survivor, she'd proven that, but it was a little unnerving to think of what might have happened.

Tia saw a trace of a smile on Sage's lips.

"Relax, counsellor, I was just messing with his head. My days of throwing chairs through windows are over. Can you hand me that comb?" Sage tossed her brush back into Betty's personal tack box.

Tia retrieved the grooming tool, relieved.

Sage flicked a glance at Tia. "Remember Emma said no John would pay for my skinny ass? When I said I'd never sold myself, that was true, but what I didn't say was that before I was busted for shoplifting, I was seriously thinking about it. I never got that bad, but it was freakin' close."

As she listened to Sage's confession, Tia said a silent prayer of thanks that it hadn't come to that. "I like your new choices better. I'm proud of you, Sage. You're going to make it." She reached into her shirt pocket. "In fact, once we start working on this ..." She took out a sheet of paper and began unfolding it. "I think things will go better for you — and not just at home and school, but everywhere. I believe that exciting career as a freelance photographer could be more than just a dream."

Sage looked confused. "What are you yakking about now?"

Tia showed her the paper. "It's a lot of technical talk, but the part that should interest you is this …" She pointed to the word *dyslexia*. "Sage, my sister has dyslexia, along with other problems. The trouble you have with reading the board and writing, forming letters backwards — when I saw those things, bells went off in my head. I kept that English paper you tossed and had my parents show it to my sister's doctor. He thinks you should be tested for dyslexia."

"You mean my brain is screwed up, and that's what makes me a dummy?" Sage asked astonished.

"You're not a dummy, Sage. You have a wiring problem that scrambles signals to your brain so you don't interpret them the same as everyone else. The great thing is that you can be helped. A lot can be done for kids with dyslexia."

For once, Sage was speechless. Then she whispered, "Wait till my mom and dad hear this. It will rock their world!"

Tia heard the amazement in Sage's voice, and the hope. No kid wants to be left out in the cold for any reason. Tia suspected that, given the help she needed, Sage's temper control would improve along with her tolerance for her parents and their rules. "I think it will rock your world, too!"

Sage's face split into a wide grin. "I always knew I was brilliant, but I could never prove it!"

Tia felt as though she had won some huge contest, but Sage would take home the prize. She remembered all those years of being the kid who looked different, the one who didn't fit in. Things had changed, and now she could change them for others who didn't fit in. Now she would help others see that they could fit in, that we all do somewhere, and if it isn't exactly with the rest of the herd, that's okay too. Sage would never be a follower, but that didn't mean she couldn't be a leader.

"How about you?" Sage looked at her expectantly. "Are you going to get help with those little problems you have?"

"What are you talking about?" Tia said defensively. "I don't have any problems, little or big."

Sage shook her head. "Denial, common symptom. I'm surprised a bright trail rider like you couldn't spot the clues." She began to list them on her fingers. "You freak if you don't get your thousand stupid crunches in or run your marathon everyday. You won't sleep until you get your paper work done, even if it means staying up all night. And you're an absolute Tidy Tyrant! That day in the barn when you were rushing around picking up everyone else's stuff. Come on, you couldn't stand it when your stapler fell over! You, Ms. Tia Winter, have a serious virus in your hard drive." She laid a sisterly hand on Tia's shoulder. "Girlfriend, do us all a favour and get a good shrink!"

Tia felt like she'd been hit with a sledgehammer. She stared at Sage, and as the words sunk in, a door in her mind opened and the truth stampeded out, nearly knocking her over. If a client had exhibited the same behaviour she had, Tia would send her to be evaluated for OCD, Obsessive Compulsive Disorder. All the symptoms were there — she was textbook! She should have realized how bad it was the night of the dance. She'd been so crazy to finish her work that she'd neglected her first duty, which was Sage.

"Okay," she admitted slowly. "You may have a point. I will take that under advisement and get back to you." She kept her tone light, but in her heart she knew Sage had seen something she'd been denying for a long time.

"You said you had a sister who has health problems. What's the matter with her?" Sage gently combed the mare's silky mane.

"Ah, she's severely handicapped physically." Tia wondered where Sage was going with this. "Motor control stuff, and she has some learning problems — dyslexia for one. My folks have devoted their lives to working with her." A warm look came into Tia's eyes. "I love the little fighter. She's a great kid."

"But she needs a lot of work, *a lot of looking after*." Sage went on like a junior psychologist. "I bet you want to make life easier for your parents by not needing *any* help — always great grades, enrolled in university early, an A student, and in perfect shape physically. Toss that into your psycho-stew and see what gets served up."

185

Tia was amazed at the girl's ability to see what others hadn't. Still, it was a hard pill to swallow. It's easy to point the finger at someone else and say, "you need help," but when it's yourself, you never truly see that person looking back at you in the mirror. Tia hugged Sage. "I really will talk to someone. You may be a screwed-up runaway kid from the streets …" There was a mischievous twinkle in her eye. "But occasionally, even you get things right. And now, what about a little ride?"

Sage looked shocked. "I just got Betty looking beautiful, maybe even perfect! I don't want her getting all messed up and sweaty!"

Tia raised her eyebrows skeptically. "I think you have a few unresolved issues yourself, Doctor." As she said this, she glanced at the tack box and noticed that the leather strap from the brush Sage had tossed in was sticking out. She reached down to tuck the strap back inside, then stopped, her hand midway to the box.

Tia and Sage looked at each other. Both knew they had a long way to go. Tia shrugged and smiled. Sage grinned, then giggled. Suddenly, both Tia and Sage laughed as though they shared some incredibly funny joke.